As a dad of four, I can say firsthand, this book and the series to come will be a new family favorite.

BROCK EASTMAN, author of the Quest for Truth series

From the pen of Amanda Cleary Eastep comes *Jack vs. the Tornado* and *The Hunt for Fang*, the first two titles in an exciting new middle-grade series. Relevant, readable, and entertaining, the Tree Street Kids will resonate with young readers everywhere who enjoy stories of fun, friendship, faith, adventure, and humor.

GLENYS NELLIST, author of the Love Letters from God and Little Mole series

The Tree Street Kids series is full of adventure and is a flat-out good read! As a young reader, I grabbed a book that encouraged my faith and devoured it. I think the same thing will happen as children read this series. Bravo!

CHRIS FABRY, author and host of Chris Fabry Live on Moody Radio

As a mom of three, I am constantly trying to find good books for my kids that are full of adventure, yet not too scary. It makes me so happy to have found the Tree Street Kids series—my kids (and I) can't wait to read more!

ISABEL TOM, mom and author of *The Value of Wrinkles: A Young Perspective on How Loving the Old Will Change Your Life*

The Hunt for Fang is another thrilling adventure from author Amanda Cleary Eastep. Follow the neighborhood kids as they learn team building and survival skills that they unexpectedly have to put to good use. From an adventure in the deep woods to a warm narrative of a boy and his dog, your children will be on the edge of their seats as they turn the pages of this delightful book. A sweet story about friendship and love reaches an unforgettable conclusion that involves a surprise gift and the providence of God. Get this book and this series—I promise, you won't regret it, and your children will thank you.

RAY RHODES JR., author of *Susie: The Life and Legacy of Susannah Spurgeon* and *Yours, till Heaven: The Untold Love Story of Charles and Susie Spurgeon*

The Tree Street Kids will be one of those book series you and your kids want to read again and again. These neighborhood kids are so funny and real and engaging; they seem like they might just live next door. I loved tagging along as they tackled big adventures and grappled with real-life situations. As a Christian parent, I treasure books that tell great stories *and* point children to God. Yes, both things are possible, and Amanda does it well. Enjoy!

JAMIE JANOSZ, managing editor, Today in the Word; author, *When Others Shuddered: Eight Women Who Refused to Give Up*

The 1990s kids in the Tree Street Kids series are relatable, and their challenges are things kids in the 2020s face as well. Amanda writes with curiosity, honesty, and warmth, and has created a memorable set of characters that'll hook even reluctant readers. I'm excited that these books will make their way into a world in need of messages of faith, hope, and friendship.

MICHELLE VAN LOON, author of *Becoming Sage: Cultivating Meaning, Purpose, and Spirituality in Midlife*

Jack, Midge, and the other Tree Street Kids are the neighbors you wish you had. Each chapter is filled with adventure, fun, and friendship.

MARIANNE HERING, coauthor of the Imagination Station series

THE HUNT FOR FANG

AMANDA CLEARY EASTEP

MOODY PUBLISHERS
CHICAGO

Scriptures taken from the Holy Bible, New International Version®, NIV®. Copyright © 1973, 1978, 1984, 2011 by Biblica, Inc.™ Used by permission of Zondervan. All rights reserved worldwide. www.zondervan.com The "NIV" and "New International Version" are trademarks registered in the United States Patent and Trademark Office by Biblica, Inc.™

Although the Tree Street Kids series is set in the 1990s (with occasional references to decades prior), these books use the 2011 NIV translation when quoting Scripture.

All emphasis in Scripture has been added.

Edited by Marianne Hering
Interior Design: Erik M. Peterson and Brandi Davis
Cover and interior illustrations: Aedan Peterson
Cover design: Erik M. Peterson
Cover icon of street sign copyright © 2018 by -VICTOR- / iStock (1030917706). All rights reserved.

Library of Congress Cataloging-in-Publication Data

Names: Eastep, Amanda Cleary, author.
Title: The hunt for Fang / Amanda Cleary Eastep.
Description: Chicago : Moody Publishers, [2021] | Series: Tree street kids
 ; 2 | Audience: Ages 8-12. | Audience: Grades 4-6. | Summary: Using
 survival skills learned at a church camp, ten-year-old Jack and his
 friends go into a massive forest preserve to stop a coyote from
 threatening pets in their Chicago suburb.
Identifiers: LCCN 2020047259 (print) | LCCN 2020047260 (ebook) | ISBN
 9780802421036 (paperback) | ISBN 9780802499134 (ebook)
Subjects: CYAC: Adventure and adventurers--Fiction. | Brothers and
 sisters--Fiction. | Friendship--Fiction. | Christian life--Fiction. |
 Pets--Fiction. | Coyote--Fiction.
Classification: LCC PZ7.1.E258 Hun 2021 (print) | LCC PZ7.1.E258 (ebook)
 | DDC [Fic]--dc23
LC record available at https://lccn.loc.gov/2020047259
LC ebook record available at https://lccn.loc.gov/2020047260

Printed by: Bethany Press in Bloomington, MN, February 2021

Originally delivered by fleets of horse-drawn wagons, the affordable paperbacks from D. L. Moody's publishing house resourced the church and served everyday people. Now, after more than 125 years of publishing and ministry, Moody Publishers' mission remains the same—even if our delivery systems have changed a bit. For more information on other books (and resources) created from a biblical perspective, go to www.moodypublishers .com or write to:

Moody Publishers
820 N. LaSalle Boulevard
Chicago, IL 60610

1 3 5 7 9 10 8 6 4 2

Printed in the United States of America

To my husband, Dan,
who hung out with the Tree Street gang in New Jersey
and who never says, "No girls allowed."
I love you.

To my Grandma Jo,
who taught me to pick catnip for tea and dandelions for salad
and took me on my first walk in the woods.
I miss you.

CONTENTS

1

A HOWL IN THE NIGHT

The howl woke me up.

Actually, it was more of a screeching *eeeooh-eeeooh-EEEEEE-ooh!*

I sat bolt upright and banged my head into the low slanted ceiling over the right side of my bed. "Ow!" So much for my nice dream about hitting the tie-breaking home run.

I'd hit my head about a hundred times since we moved from the farmhouse to King's Grove in the suburbs at the beginning of summer.

I glanced sideways at my purple Nickelodeon Time Blaster clock. For now, it sat on a folding chair on the unslanty-ceiling side of my bed. The goo-green numbers glowed 4:00 a.m. At 6:30 sharp on school days, it would

sing out: "Nick-nick-nick-nick-nick-nick-nick-nick-nick-
uh-lo-dee-uhnnn!" The first day at my new school, August
29, 1995, was only a couple weeks away.

I flopped back onto my pillow, just as something white
with black spots and the size of my little sister hurtled
through the gray dark. She landed—all pointy knees and
elbows—right onto my belly.

"*Oof!*" The wind rushed out of me.

The howl must have woken up Midge, too, who was
dressed in her favorite 101 Dalmatian pajamas.

Apparently, the Foolproof Anti-Sister Room Alarm I'd
rigged up wasn't so foolproof. Sheesh. Little sisters are no
respecters of territorial boundaries.

"Did you hear that, Jack?" she whisper-screamed into
my face.

I could smell her morning breath. And chocolate. How
Midge always manages to smell like a Tootsie Roll, I have
no idea.

"It came from the cem-e-terrryyy!"

Adams Cemetery is on the corner, and our new house is
the first house on the block and right next door to the old
graveyard, the most ancient tombstones jutting out of the
grass like jagged bottom teeth.

Even though both of our bedrooms are in the attic,
Midge's room was technically about ten feet closer to whatever was out there. I know there's no such things as ghosts.

And there definitely aren't wolves in the suburbs of Chicago.

I shoved her off. Kicking and flailing, I untangled myself from the sheet and scrambled into the dormer window—what my dad calls a doghouse. The window juts out of the slanted ceiling right beside my bed. There's plenty of room for a guy to sit and do important man thinking.

"*Yes*, the doghouse!" Midge squished in beside me.

So much for plenty of room.

My second-story window looks out over Cherry Avenue. From here, I mostly see bushy treetops. But I can also see the streetlamp standing kitty-corner to my right where Cherry makes a T with Oak Street—my friend Ellison's street. The sidewalk below—heading right—eventually dead ends at the forest preserve. And—heading left—it leads to the cemetery next door.

I slid the top window sash down.

We pressed our faces against the screen. The air smelled like musty metal and wet grass.

Another sound echoed from farther away. A racket of *yeee-ooowwwls* scratched like fingernails over the dark.

"Ghosts." Midge's voice vibrated the screen.

All my life (I was already ten as of June 2), we'd lived with my grandparents on their farm in Goodnow. I was used to the sound of stray dogs howling at night. Sometimes packs of them roamed the fields. Sometimes they snatched chickens. Before I'd go to bed, I would always make sure my pet chicken, Henrietta, was locked up safe in the coop.

These howls were different. They sounded almost . . . human.

Midge tugged my arm. "Can we catch a ghost, puhleeezzz? After all, Mom said you can't have a dog. She didn't say anything about ghosts."

I tried to imagine playing fetch with a ghost. But I was still working on convincing my mom how much I needed a *dog*.

Maybe a stray dog was outside, searching for a nice kid like me—smart (no matter what fourth grade math said). Good throwing arm. Nice to animals.

I imagined he'd have sticky-outy fur around his snout and ears and over his eyes. He'd be white with splotches of brown and black. Or black with splotches of white and brown. He'd sit next to me in the window seat—right where Midge was still yanking on my arm and begging to go investigate. When I'd say "Good, um, Snickers? . . . Rex? . . . Spot?" he'd nuzzle my hand with his wet nose. And he'd be one of those dogs that looks like they're smiling at you when they pant.

That settled it. "Fine," I said, shaking my arm free. I crawled out of the window seat and over my bed. "Let's go catch . . . whatever is out there."

Midge whisper-howled in agreement.

2

THE GRAY GHOST

We crept around the end of the tall wooden fence that divided our side yard from the cemetery. We stood there in our pajamas, like weirdos, in the cool, dewy grass at the corner of the graveyard.

The fifteen or so rows of tombstones glowed in the hazy light of the streetlamp where the sidewalk ended at the corner of Cherry and Main. I strained my eyes, searching for—I didn't know what.

Some of the tombstones stood tall and shiny with clear words and dates carved into them. Others jutted out of the ground like nubby, chipped teeth.

Midge shivered behind me. Her death grip on the back of my superhero pajama shirt felt way less annoying than

it would have in the daylight. Not that Midge wouldn't come through in a pinch. She was "scrappy" (Grandma's words). But also prone to a left hook "not befitting a Christian young lady" (Dad's words).

I crept ahead, and Midge stuck to my back like a wet leaf. My bare toes caught in the long wet grass, and I lurched ahead. Luckily, there were lots of grave markers to break a guy's fall. I grabbed the edge of an arched tombstone worn smooth on the edges, like the other ones that were so old you couldn't read the names.

I wished I had my camping lantern, but it was in the fort I shared with my friends, the Tree Street Kids. The lantern light might have spooked the gray shadow slinking behind the last row of tombstones at the back of the cemetery.

"Jack, what's that?" Midge pointed at it.

A dark, dog-shaped shadow peeked around the edge of the tombstone. The yellow eyes stared right back at me. And it definitely wasn't smiling at us.

I had never seen one in real life, but I knew what it was: a coyote. I figured it had come from Crooked Creek Woods, the massive forest preserve north of our neighborhood. It'd probably been letting its family know where it was.

Which was more than I could say for me and Midge. If I let Midge get eaten, I'd be grounded for life. I needed to figure something out. And fast—

Midge jumped out from behind me. "BOO!" she shouted

at the animal. She waved her spaghetti-noodle arms over her head. "I'm the ghost of Christmas presents!"

I yanked her back behind me just as the yellow eyes blinked out. The shadow spun around. The coyote was blocked by the fence, and Midge and I were standing smack between him and his path back to the woods.

Panicked, he sprinted toward us . . . then, *whoosh*, in a flash of gray fur, he darted past us and around the end of the tall fence.

We spun around, tripping and scrambling our way back to the sidewalk.

The coyote was already a blur, disappearing down Cherry toward the woods.

"Were you trying to get eaten?" I grabbed Midge by the hand. We needed to get back into the house before Mom and Dad woke up. "And it's the Ghost of Christmas *Present*, not presents."

Midge skipped to keep up as I hauled her down the sidewalk, past the end of our driveway, and across our side yard.

"You're supposed to make yourself look big and scary when you see a coyote."

Midge tosses out science-y facts like I do empty candy wrappers.

"Maybe you just looked like a bigger snack," I said. "Besides, coyotes should stay in the woods where they belong."

"Maybe he didn't want to move to the suburps, either," she said. "Just like you."

"It's su*burbs*, not burps," I said, instead of admitting she might be right.

We hurried across the dewy grass, the bottoms of my pajama pants plastered to my ankles.

The sunrise was smearing pink across the sky. Mom and Dad would be awake any second. We scrambled up the back porch steps and halted at the back door.

"Shhh! Don't make a peep." I slowly pulled open the squeaky screen door. I turned the doorknob and carefully pushed open the back door.

The smell of coffee whacked me in the face.

"Uh-oh!" Midge said. "Smells like trouble."

We tiptoed up into the kitchen.

Yep. Even bigger trouble than Dad being awake.

Mom stood at the counter, about to take a sip of coffee. Calmly, she turned and glared at us through the steam rising from her cup.

The light of the fluorescent bulb over the coffeepot twitched across her face.

After just being in the cemetery, I imagined the whole scenario might have looked like a spooky *Goosebumps* episode. Except this was real-life scary. You get grounded in real life.

She took a long sip and closed her eyes. Without even opening them she said: "Okay. In ten words or less, please."

Before I could build a short, punishment-proof, mom-acceptable answer—

"Catching coyotes!" Midge blurted.

Mom's eyes got crazy wide.

How do moms do that? I don't ever want to *see* the eyes in the *back* of their heads.

Dad shuffled into the kitchen and straight to the coffeepot. "Moor-in," he mumbled, behind Mom. He poured coffee into the "Daddy Saurus-rex" mug Midge had given him for his birthday three years ago. Then he turned and squinted over Mom's shoulder. "Why are you two up"—he took a slurp of coffee—"and covered in grass?"

"We were in the ceme—" Midge started.

I reached around the back of her head and clamped my hand over her mouth. "We heard a noise."

Midge licked my palm.

Blech. That always made me let go. I wiped my hand on my already trashed pajama pants.

"It was a coyote hiding behind the tombstones!" She dropped to her knees, raised her head, and let loose an irritating—but impressive—yowl.

"Jack, I know how much you've been wanting a dog, but we just can't adopt the local wildlife." Dad chuckled at his coyote joke.

Mom didn't.

This seemed a perfect time to change the subject. "So, Dad . . . speaking of dogs . . ."

"What if that animal had attacked you?" Mom asked, ignoring my excellent segue.

Midge crawled to mom on all fours. She wagged her pretend tail and pretended to beg.

Mom absentmindedly petted Midge's head.

I wondered if I acted like a dog if I'd be in less trouble.

"It could have had rabies. Do you know how painful rabies shots are? Do you know how long the needle is?"

Mom always knows just what to say to make a kid sorry for ever stalking wild animals in cemeteries at 4:00 a.m.

"I'm talking to you too, ma'am." She simultaneously snapped and pointed at Midge. (Another cool Mom trick.)

"This isn't the country, kids," Dad said, yawning. "There's busy roads and far more people and thousands of acres of forest preserve. Not tractors and cows and cornfields. The suburbs are a different world."

That was for sure. Compared to the country, the suburbs were Jupiter.

"You kids get cleaned up," Dad said. "As long as we're all up, I'll start the pancakes."

My chance to focus my parents' minds on a furry, loving, loyal, and very tame pet streaked away, just like the elusive coyote.

3

WATER BUFFALO PANCAKES

Saturday is my favorite day. Even in the summer. That's when Dad is usually home from his out-of-town construction job. Being closer to his work sites was why we'd moved at the beginning of the summer. Plus, my grandparents were selling the farmhouse.

We'd had a dog at the farm, but he died last year. Hutch was a big old mutt. He was already ten when I was born in 1985, and I turned ten this past June. (Wow, I'm almost doing math!) It would have been fun if Hutch and I could have celebrated our birthdays together—twenty dog bones on his cake and ten trick candles on mine.

I tried lots of times to teach him to fetch. I'd throw an old baseball into the cornfield. Hutch would come back with—yuck!—a mouse or a mole.

I bet a suburban dog wouldn't do that. He'd eat dog food from a can. He would sit, roll over, play dead, and actually fetch a ball.

I have a list of dog names ready, just in case.

Shadow
Chance
Lucky
Lord Zedd

And not so favorite names . . .

Snickers
(Dad's suggestion, after his favorite candy bar)
Barky, Waggy, Woofy, Furry, and T. rex
(Midge's suggestions)

The other reason I love Saturdays—Dad makes his famous people pancakes, which are basically pancakes in the shape of us.

I changed and hurried back downstairs.

Dad was already drizzling pancake batter into the skillet.

"Dad, wait!" I stopped him before he could make a pancake shaped like me mowing the lawn. "Can you make me a German Shepherd?"

He pointed the spatula at me like a magic wand. "Zap! You're a German Shepherd."

"That's a good one, Dad." I stood next to him and watched the creamy batter trickle off the tip of the spoon and stick to the hot pan.

Rectangular body.

Four legs. A tail.

A head . . . I think.

And horns? Or maybe ears. Three of them.

"Hm. It'll look better when I flip it," he said.

I watched the raw batter bubble.

Midge skipped into the kitchen, still wearing her soggy pj's. She poked her head between me and Dad.

"*Ooo*, I want a water buffalo too!"

"It's a *dog*." I pressed the tip of my finger into her forehead and pushed.

She didn't go away.

"Or maybe a cow," Dad said. He slid the spatula under the pancake and carefully flipped it over.

"Definitely a dog," I argued. "I like that he has three ears. He'll have supersonic hearing."

"And give milk," Midge added.

Mom appeared in the kitchen just catching the end of the conversation. "There's milk in the fridge."

"We were talking about Jack's cow," Dad clarified. He scooped up my pancake and slid it onto the top plate of the stack on the counter.

"Water buffalo," said Midge.

"Dooog." I grabbed my plate and stalked to the kitchen table. Why was getting a dog so difficult in this house?

"If Jack is getting a dog," Midge said, taking my spot next to Dad, "I want four frogs."

"You can have one frog . . ." Dad said to Midge. Batter sizzled as it hit the pan.

I poured a puddle of syrup under my pancake dog.

"Then I'll cook more after you eat the first one."

"I don't want frogs to eat!" Midge laughed. (I swear she laughs like a super evil cartoon villain.) "I want real frogs. For pets. Specifically *Pseudacris triseriata.*"[1]

"Hey," I said, stuffing half the cow-dog in my mouth, "how about a *pseudacris ludicrous*?"

Mom sat at the table with her refilled coffee cup and her Bible. "How about you take your sister frog hunting in the creek this morning?"

I sighed. Sometimes witty brother humor just doesn't pay.

"As fun as that would be," I said, trying to sound disappointed, "Ellison and I are outfitting the bomb shelter today."

Even though my new friends Ellison, Roger, and Ruthie

call us the Tree Street Kids, we don't have a tree house. We just all live on streets named for trees.

Roger Jennings lives on Pine. Ruthie Galinski lives on Maple. Ellison Henry lives on Oak, the street I can see from my window.

And I live on Cherry. Which is a fruit, but also a tree. That makes me (okay, and Midge) part of the group.

Our actual fort is next door in an underground bomb shelter in Mr. Bruno's backyard.

"That bomb shelter has been there since the 1960s," Mom said. "After thirty-plus years, there's no rush to decorate it."

"We're not *decorating*. We're outfitting. You know, with survival supplies."

But Mom wasn't going to let me off easy. Especially after the early morning coyote adventure. "Sounds like a plan," she said, opening her Bible. "Family devotions, frog hunting, and then not-decorating."

4

THE FROG HUNT

Ellison was all in for a frog hunt. Hearing about our coyote encounter may have sparked his adventurous side. Plus, he's a pretty agreeable guy and the best friend I made after moving to the suburbs, even though we're kinda different.

He reads books. I read video game magazines.

He has a short flattop. I have straight brown hair my mom shaves off in the summer.

He wears glasses. I can read the bottom line of the eye chart at school.

He likes to pitch. I play shortstop.

He's memorized, like, half of the Bible. I've memorized "Jesus wept."

Outside, the three of us hopped onto our bikes.

"I'll show you the coolest spot in the park," Ellison said. "You'll definitely catch a frog there."

We rode up Cherry and braked at the stop sign.

"Wait!" Midge said. She was wearing her red-and-black ladybug backpack and matching rain boots and my old Teenage Mutant Ninja Turtles bike helmet. It was bright green with big eyes behind a purple mask. Midge was kind of obsessed with reptilian superheroes since Mom had signed her up for karate classes at the park and rec center.

She turned her head to the right, all four of her eyes staring down Maple Street toward the park. "I've never been past the stop sign without Mom."

"Welcome to the edge of the world," I said.

"'Where the wild wind whirled . . .'" Ellison added, dramatically. He is always quoting books.

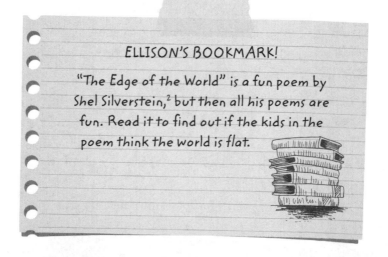

ELLISON'S BOOKMARK!

"The Edge of the World" is a fun poem by Shel Silverstein,[2] but then all his poems are fun. Read it to find out if the kids in the poem think the world is flat.

"The world is round. That has been proven," Midge said, seeming not totally convinced.

"Our neighborhood is flat," I said. I pointed toward the park. "Frog Paradise." Next, I pointed behind us toward home. "The castle." I swept my arm wide to the left and the three blocks where Ruthie, Roger, and Ellison lived on Maple, Pine, and Oak. "Tree Street Kids territory. And, here"—I lowered my voice and pointed ahead of us where the forest preserve stretched for miles—"be dragons."

I like to draw maps. On really old maps, dragons meant dangerous or uncharted territory. Since moving here, I've drawn some maps of the neighborhood.

I hadn't explored the woods yet, so in my last map that part was marked by a cool dragon in the middle of some leafy scribbles. I'd have to add a coyote now.

"Dragons . . . sure," Midge said, tightening the strap on the big green helmet. "Let's start small."

Ellison nodded toward the park. "Onward to Frog Paradise!" he shouted.

The park bordered the forest preserve and was dotted with huge trees. It was like the woods didn't know where they were supposed to end.

We passed little kids swinging and climbing the monkey bars. Bigger kids shooting hoops on the cracked asphalt basketball court. A guy throwing a Frisbee to his dog, who caught it in midair.

I wanted to stop and pet the dog, but we were on a mission to get Midge her own pet.

We pedaled through the grass to the edge of an embankment. At the bottom, a creek trickled along the far border of the park. Just ahead from where we stood, the creek disappeared beneath a stone bridge and into the woods. We laid our bikes on the grass and climbed down the small hill to the water.

Midge dropped the helmet and her ladybug backpack onto the ground. She pulled an empty pickle jar and my old goldfish net out of the backpack and set them in the grass.

"Why do you want *four* frogs?" I asked.

"So I can name them Michelangelo, Leonardo, Raphael, and Donatello." She squatted into a karate warrior stance, her pretzel-stick legs wide and her little fists locked and loaded at her sides.

"The Ninja Turtles are *turtles*, not frogs." I think that was the first time I'd corrected her on biology.

She karate punched the air. "They're like frogs with armor."

"I usually see them along the bank or near the foot of the bridge," Ellison said. He rolled up his jeans, slid off his shoes and socks, and set them neatly beside each other on the sparse grass.

We stepped closer to the shallow water. Our feet squelched in the mud. The water was darker under the shade from the bridge and the trees along the bank. Spots of sun spotlighted tiny darting minnows. It smelled like a classroom fish tank.

"Okay, we need to be quiet if we want to catch a frog," I said, leaning carefully over the water.

Lacey green moss floated along the pebbly bank.

"Sneaky . . . stealthy . . ." I whispered.

A pair of bulbous eyes peeked through the moss right in front of us.

"There's a big one!" Ellison said.

The eyes disappeared in a blink. With a squeak of alarm, it leaped away into the shadows of the trestle bridge.

But it didn't matter, Midge followed him into the ankle-deep water, slapping wildly with the fish net.

Not the best plan. But Ellison and I sloshed in after her. Stealth was useless now.

We slipped and scrambled on the slimy rocks, trying to get some traction. We got our balance and scanned the creek.

"Don't move," Ellison whispered, pointing at my feet.

Midge turned toward us, tiny net at the ready.

Sitting right at the toes of my soaked gym shoes was a glossy green frog the size of my hand.

"Grab him!" Midge hollered.

Ellison and I lunged for it at the same time.

The frog hopped out of the water again, back legs dangling as it flew through the air toward Midge.

Ellison and I slammed into each other and fell into the creek.

Midge dropped her net and tried to catch the slippery blob in midair.

Grab, *slip*, grab, *squish* . . . and PLOP! Back into the creek as Midge slipped and fell on top of us.

About three feet away, and nearly under the bridge now, the frog sat staring at us.

"We need a bigger net," I said, as we pushed ourselves up and stared back at him.

And just like that, a huge net at the end of a long handle swung down and scooped up the frog.

5

SAVE DONATELLO!

A tall kid—at least he looked tall from where we sat—appeared out of the shadows of the trestle bridge. His dark hair hung in his eyes. He was dressed in military boots and green-and-brown camouflage.

No wonder we hadn't seen him.

He dropped the net handle and sloshed toward us. Then he grabbed up the net, twisting it so the frog was trapped at the bottom in a muddy lump.

"That's how you catch a frog, nerds." He laughed, his teeth showing like a dog when it doesn't want you in its yard. He made his way out of the creek.

"Oh, no," Ellison mumbled, as we staggered up and

tried to look less nerdy. "Tree Street Kids enemy number one—Buzz Rublatz."

"That's my frog!" Midge yelped, hopping up. "His name is Donatello."

Buzz stopped on the bank and turned around. "This is *my* frog. His name is *lunch* . . . for my snake."

Croak? The frog struggled in the net.

Buzz kicked Midge's pickle jar and ladybug backpack into the water. "And this park and these woods"—he swept his pointy finger in a full circle above his head—"are my territory."

He started up the hill with the net and, um, lunch.

"Hey, you can't do that," Ellison called, pushing up his mud-splattered glasses. "And this is a *public* park. Everyone shares!"

Obviously Buzz believed he *could* do that. But I had to give Ellison kudos for trying.

"*Here* be dragons . . ." Ellison grumbled. He waded out of the creek and picked up the wet backpack and pickle jar on the way.

I grabbed Midge's hand and we followed. "We'll find a bigger frog later," I told her, watching Buzz stride easily up the embankment.

As soon as we were out of the water, Midge screeched, "Save Donatello!" She snatched up her bike helmet and strapped it on, then she chased the kid up the hill.

I'm not a wimp, but I'm not a fan of confrontation. I don't go looking for trouble. And Buzz looked like trouble.

I hurried after my sister, my gym shoes squishing water out as I scrambled uphill. I reached the top, and there was Midge, face-to-face with Buzz. Well, face-to-frog anyway.

Buzz held out the handle so that the net full of frog and muck was right under Midge's nose. "Jaws is gonna looove this juicy frog," he teased.

When Midge grabbed for the net, he raised it far above her head.

"Knock it off," I said. It came out way nicer than I meant it to.

A chipped front tooth showed as Buzz's lip curled up. "Suuurrre," he said, keeping his eyes on Midge. He pulled the long handle back but grabbed hold of the frog, net and all.

It let loose a squeal that sounded like a cross between a squeaky dog toy and Ellison's baby sister, Maya, when she's hungry. And wet. And tired.

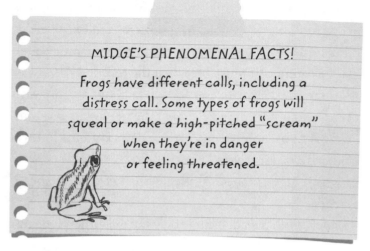

MIDGE'S PHENOMENAL FACTS!

Frogs have different calls, including a distress call. Some types of frogs will squeal or make a high-pitched "scream" when they're in danger or feeling threatened.

"You're hurting it!" Midge cried.

Ellison came up behind me just as I was about to launch myself at Buzz.

Except, at that very second, Midge stepped up to him, crouched into her warrior stance, and pulled her fists back at her sides.

"Midge, no!" Ellison and I both yelled.

Too late. Her right fist shot out and landed a small but mighty punch into Buzz's belly.

"Oof!" He dropped the net, frog and all, and clutched his stomach.

Midge snatched up the net, handle dragging behind, and ran back to the edge of the embankment. "Be free, Donatello!"

Apparently, our frog hunt was about to become a frog rescue.

Midge shook the frog out of the net and onto the grass. She gave him a gentle shove down the hill.

"It's just a dumb frog," Buzz said.

I looked back at Buzz.

He glared at me. His face was red, from anger or embarrassment, I wasn't sure. "I know you," he growled. "You're the new kid. You live next to the *cemetery*."

He said the word like maybe the *cemetery* was a convenient spot for when he eventually got his revenge.

Where was a witty comeback when you needed one?

Or even a dramatic book quote. Ellison just stood next to me wearing Midge's sopping wet ladybug backpack and holding the pickle jar and his still clean shoes and socks.

"Yeahhh," I drawled, glaring back at Buzz. "That's *my* territory."

"Good one," Ellison whispered.

Buzz just scowled.

Midge ran up to me, and I grabbed her slimy hand. The three of us hurried past Buzz and headed back to our bikes.

It wasn't even lunchtime, and this day had me beat.

Jack: 0

Local wildlife (counting the coyote and Buzz): 2

Mom was yanking weeds from between the cracks of the front walk when we rode up to the house. She glanced up from her attack on a huge dandelion. Her eyes got wide when she saw us. "What in the world . . . ?"

We were soaked, muddy, and frogless. Plus, Midge looked like she was about to bawl her eyes out. She gets like that when she's mad. Or she's done something she shouldn't have.

Not waiting for an answer, Mom clapped the dirt from her hands, stood up, and marched us over to the garage where Dad had his head under the hood of the truck.

"Family meeting," Mom said in her scary-chipper voice.

Before I could explain, the whole story spilled out of Midge.

"Midge." Dad squatted down and cupped her face in his leathery hand.

Her lip trembled and she sniffed a big goober up just as it started to form a really impressive bubble out of her left nostril.

"What have I told you to do if someone picks on you?"

Midge sniffed again but brightened up. "Hit 'em and ask questions later."

Ooo! Wrong answer.

Dad's eyes got wide, and he shot a look at Mom. She glared back at him and shook her head.

"Oh," Midge mumbled, "I guess that was Grandma."

Grandma wasn't about to get grounded. But Midge was. No frog hunting—or even rescuing—for the next week. It would have been longer, but Mom said Midge *was* trying to save the frog, after all.

I didn't point out that before that she'd been trying to trap it in a pickle jar.

6

THE DOG PRAYER

After Saturday's wildlife adventures, I was ready for a trip back to the farm. Starting with church with Grandpa Ernie and Grandma Josephine.

My shirt collar and Sonic the Hedgehog clip-on tie made my neck itch. But the itchy torture was worth it. We were back in our old town for only the second time this summer. Grandpa wore a suit coat and Grandma smelled like lilacs. Being in church all together almost felt like Christmas.

I even heard everything the pastor said about God creating the world. How He made people to rule over the fish in the sea and the birds in the sky and every creature that moves on the ground.[3] That got me thinking about dogs, which made me think of bones, which made me think of Grandma's fried chicken and biscuits.

Bruuhhbloop. Never think of Sunday dinner on an empty stomach in a quiet church when everyone is praying. I pressed the hymnal over my belly to muffle the growling. *Grrrrrweeep.*

Grandpa handed me a red-and-white star mint.

I'd have to wait till everyone was belting out "All Creatures of Our God and King" before unwrapping the crackly cellophane. So I prayed until then.

I thanked God that we were back in our old town. (Don't thank God for fried chicken and biscuits. Don't thank God for fried chicken and . . .) And then I decided to ask Him something I wasn't so sure I should pray about. *Jesus, I don't know if You had a pet as a kid, like maybe a goat. I hear they make good watchdogs. And as long as we're talking about dogs, You know how much I'd really, really, realllyyy like to have a dog . . .*

The church and my old school sit right at the very edge of town. Kind of like a fortress with the village behind it and a sea of cornfields to the west. The white steeple was always the first thing I'd see when we'd drive from the farmhouse into town.

After church, all the grown-ups huddled in groups in the parking lot. They always tell us kids it's time to go home.

But then the men start talking about the Chicago Cubs baseball season. The women start talking about—actually, I have no idea—probably babies and stuff. So all us kids head straight for the school playground.

Except now I was ten. I thought maybe I'd try hanging with the men and talk about Sammy Sosa's runs batted in. Dad was still disappointed I decided not to play youth league baseball in our new town this summer. But I had a good lawn-mowing business going, a new fort to outfit (not decorate!), and new friends (and maybe an enemy).

I was sitting on the tailgate of Grandpa's Ford Bronco. He and Dad and a few men in itchy-looking shirts loosened their ties and talked and laughed. Sometimes I laughed even if I didn't know what was so funny. Finally, Grandma—in a cloud of lilac perfume and determination—came to the rescue of my still growling stomach.

"Morning, men," she said, kind of like a drill sergeant. "Ernie"—she smiled real big at Grandpa—"the chicken isn't going to fry itself."

Grandpa smoothed a hand over his tuft of reddish gray hair. "It definitely wouldn't do as good a job as you, dear."

The men all shook hands like you do at the end of a baseball game and headed off to their own families.

Mom had retrieved Midge from the monkey bars, where she usually hangs upside down from the knees pretending to be a bat. She also wants to be a biologist. (Dad says there's a fine line between studying animals and wanting to be one.)

As my family started piling into the Bronco, I helped Grandpa shut the tailgate. "Grandpa," I said, kind of quiet since the Bronco's tailgate window wasn't rolled up yet, "did you ever pray for something you *wanted*?"

Grandpa grabbed one end of his loose tie and pulled it through his collar.

I unclipped my Sonic tie.

He winked. "I got your Grandma Josephine, didn't I?"

I followed him around the side of the Bronco. "I was thinking more like a Labrador-German-Shepherd mix that fetches and doesn't pee in the house."

Grandpa stopped and rested his hand on the driver's side door handle. He looked down at me. "Seems right to pray for a companion . . . why else would the Lord invent dogs?"

I nodded. I liked that God invented stuff like I do sometimes. (Which reminded me that I needed to fix that Anti-Sister Room Alarm.)

"They have four legs so they can keep up with children," he added as he swung open the door.

That didn't really explain cows or water buffalo, but I knew what he meant.

Before I climbed into the back seat with Mom, Grandma, and Midge, I finished the prayer I'd started inside the church. I hoped God would hear it just as well outside.

"What Grandpa said. Every kid needs a pet. And if You could send a frog Midge's way, she'd really like that."

"Rarf, rarf!" I could almost hear my dog barking now. Except I wasn't imagining it!

"Rarf, rarf!" A real live bark sounded in the distance. Grandpa jumped back out of the driver's seat and pointed at the cornfield behind me.

I spun around and looked out at the field.

Something rustled the green leaves along one row of the cornstalks as the barking grew louder.

"What's taking so long? Those biscuits won't bake themselves!" Grandma hollered from inside the car. Then she and everyone else climbed out to see what was taking so long.

I watched the movement in the long green leaves come closer to the edge of the field.

A barking ball of fur, mud, and sticks shot out of the cornfield like an arrow from a bow. It headed straight for me.

Its legs were black with dirt, and its coat stuck out in weird patches.

"Puppy!" Midge screeched.

Shocked, I fell to my knees on the ground, not caring about my Sunday clothes. I opened my arms wide.

7

NO-NAME

The dog barreled into my chest, yowling and nipping and scrambling like he was happy to see me again.

I could hardly breathe. Everyone surrounded me, talking at once—I think I heard "fleas" and "rabies" at some point from Grandma and Mom and "Snickers!" from Dad.

I looked into the dog's matted and muddy face; everything seemed blurry. I didn't realize why until I wiped my arm across my eyes. I was so happy, I was crying.

Plus, that dog stunk like a garbage can on an August day. Not only did it need a haircut, but it also needed about ten bubble baths.

Midge was laughing and trying to pet the dog too while he squirmed in my arms.

"Where did you come from?" I asked.

Midge waved her hand in front of her face. "Pee-yew. I think he came from Mars. Scientists say it smells like rotten eggs."

The tail wagged so hard it slapped me in the face. His whole body wagged.

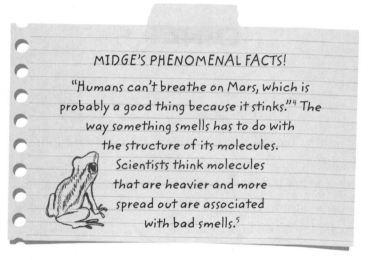

MIDGE'S PHENOMENAL FACTS!

"Humans can't breathe on Mars, which is probably a good thing because it stinks."[4] The way something smells has to do with the structure of its molecules. Scientists think molecules that are heavier and more spread out are associated with bad smells.[5]

"I'm going to name you Stinker," she said, wiping her hand on her shirt.

"I'm naming him!" I guess I said it not too nicely because Midge frowned at me.

The dog stopped wagging and wiggling. He scuttled backward out of my lap and cocked his head to the side.

I mean, I had prayed for a dog. I should pick the name.

"No one is naming him," Dad said.

"But, Dad—"

"Jack, we don't even know who he belongs to."

I hadn't thought of that. My heart fell right down to my hungry belly.

The dog stuck out its tongue, panting. He wagged his tail, oblivious to my inner turmoil.

"He sure doesn't look like he belongs to anyone," Grandpa said. "No collar."

"The fleas probably ate it," Grandma said.

I held out the back of my hand toward his wet black nose. He licked my fingers. I wondered if he could taste the Cinnamon Toast Crunch I'd eaten before church.

Midge held her hand out and he licked her fingers too. They probably tasted like the chocolate-covered caramels Grandma sneaked to her in church to keep her quiet.

"Can we keep him till we find out whose dog he is?" I scratched him behind what felt like an ear under all the fur and cockleburs.

I heard the grown-up conference going on over my head. "Stray," "lost," "call the police department and vet tomorrow," and "good scrub" . . .

Yep, so far, so good until—

"Rabies . . ."

"Lynn," Dad said to my mom, "if that dog has rabies, then so do I."

"Maybe not yet," she said.

I remembered a T-shirt Ellison wore sometimes with a WWJD on it. "Mom, 'What would Jesus do?'"

I heard a heavy sigh as she leaned over me. She patted the dog on the head and said, "He'd tell the little children to grab the soap and scissors and make a miracle happen."

"Yay!" I yelped, scaring the dog again. Oops. "Wanna go home?" I asked him. "Wanna go for a ride?"

As soon as I said "ride," the little guy went crazy. And ran away.

"No! Come back!" I shouted. But the dog hadn't run back to the cornfield. He was running in wide circles around us and the Bronco. On his next approach, he leaped through the open passenger door and into the front seat.

Before we piled back into the truck, Dad scooped the dog up and moved him and his fleas to the back of the Bronco. He happily looked out the back window as we drove back to the farmhouse.

I kept turning around in my seat to check on him during the mile-long drive from the church to the first crossroad. The farmhouse sat on an acre of crabgrass surrounded by a bazillion acres of cornfields.

While Grandma and Mom fried chicken, Grandpa scrounged up some canned dog food from the back of the pantry. He'd kept it after Hutch died, "just in case."

In the backyard of the farmhouse, I filled an empty Cool Whip container with water from the hose and glopped the food onto a paper plate.

The dog danced around my feet. I set the water and food in the grass, and he gobbled and gulped up both in a blink.

Dad helped me and Midge clip the dog's long white, brown, and black fur. He might not have had fleas, but his coat was infested with pokey cockleburs.

Midge scooped the clippings into a pile. She added burs for eyes and a twig for a mouth. A red petal from Grandma's rosebushes made a pretty decent tongue. "Ta-da! Now he has a little sister," Midge announced.

"I don't know," I said, "she's kind of quiet to be a little sister."

Midge wrinkled her nose at me and petted the ball of fluff until its rose-petal mouth fell off.

Next, Dad and I filled a metal washtub with water from the hose. Mom added a pot full of hot water to warm it up. While we scrubbed his filthy coat with Hutch's leftover flea shampoo, Midge sat at the picnic making a doghouse out of a cardboard storage box Grandma had given her. She set the box on its side and used the lid to build a pointed roof. On the back of the doghouse, she added two round windows made out of clear yogurt container lids. And she cut a mailbox slot in the short end of the box.

"Who's going to send a dog mail?" I asked, shielding myself with a beach towel as the dog shook off three baths worth of water.

"I am," Midge said, holding up a piece of paper with "I love you, No-Name" printed on it. "Or maybe whoever lost him. Except they'll need the address."

I smacked my palm to my forehead. "If the owner had the address, the dog wouldn't be lost anymore."

Midge ignored my logic. "Can we name him just for today?" she asked Dad.

He dumped the third tub of dirty bath water into the grass. "Just for today, but Grandpa will be calling the police station and the town vet in the morning to see if anyone has reported a lost pet."

He said Grandpa would put an advertisement in the town paper too. Grandpa had a theory. Since the dog liked "rides" so much, he'd probably belonged to a long-distance truck driver. Maybe the trucker had stopped to gas up or get a banana split at the Dairy-Lite on the highway. When the dog ran off, the trucker had no choice but to continue on his route.

I knew how sad I'd be if I lost such a great dog. Still, I didn't want him to be found by anyone but me. "I can draw posters that say 'FOUND, vicious attack dog, 25 cent reward.'"

"Hmm, not exactly accurate, is it?" Dad said.

"You can't blame a dogless boy for trying," Midge said.

8

TYRANNOCANIS REX

With his bad haircut and third bath, the dog looked like a drowned rat. He was way smaller than I thought. I rubbed him down with an old towel and sat beside him in the grass. The sun was bright and warm, and he fell asleep as soon as he curled himself into a furry C.

The sunshine dried his fur into long patches and bald spots.

After Midge finished the portraits she'd painted of each of us on the doghouse walls, she skipped over and sat on the other side of the dog. "What do you want to name him? Maybe I could name him today, and you could name him tomorrow." She gently patted his head between the two pointed ears with the floppy tips we'd uncovered.

I didn't want to think about tomorrow. What if Grandpa found the owner by then?

"I'm naming him *Tyrannocanis rex*," said Midge. "It's a mix of my favorite dinosaur, and *canis*, the scientific name for dogs. And Rex is already a dog name."

I looked down at him snoozing between us. When we found him this morning, he was half the size of the Lab-German-Shepherd mix I'd imagined having. After his haircut, he was now half of the half. Tyrannocanis rex seemed a little extreme.

"What name are you picking?"

The dog opened its eyes and yawned. He pressed his front paws deep into the grass, stuck his scruffy bottom in the air, and stretched. He put a paw on my knee, wagging his tattered tail like a flag. His fur had dried and stuck up in patches around the bald spots where Dad and I had cut the burs out. He looked ridiculous.

Patches? No. Scruffy? Nah.

I didn't want to name him just for tomorrow. I wanted to name him like he'd be my dog forever.

Ruffling his muzzle with my hands, I put my nose against his wet one. "What do you want your name to be?"

He barked in my face. And then he bolted, running wide circles around us.

I hopped up and whistled for him.

He hurtled toward me, just like he had out of the field that morning. Like an arrow shot from a bow. Just . . . like . . . an—

"Arrow!" I shouted the name at him.

With only a few yards to go before he reached me, he launched himself into the air and . . .

I caught him!

"Wow!" Midge yelled, jumping up. "He must've run away from the circus!"

As the dog wriggled against my chest and licked my face, I closed my eyes. I thanked God for answering my prayer. Even if Arrow would only be mine until tomorrow.

I promised-promised-promised to take care of the dog at our house until Grandpa found the owner. He said he'd report finding a lost dog first—or maybe second or third—thing in the morning.

Praying no one was looking for him probably wasn't the right thing to pray. But I still hoped it.

Mom wasn't crazy about bringing home a dog, especially since Dad had to drive back to his out-of-town job that night.

Luckily, my grandparents still had Hutch's old collar and some clothesline for a leash. The collar was frayed and had a tag that said HUTCH FINCH. But Arrow Tyrannocanis rex didn't seem to mind.

After the hour drive back home, I tied the clothesline around the ring in the collar and put it around Arrow's neck.

The suburbs are different from the country. Even in a big yard like ours, a dog has to be tied up. Probably not fun for a maybe-circus dog.

Hutch's collar was too big, even with an extra hole punched through. Arrow could probably have pulled his head out of it if he tried, but he was too excited to explore the yard and mark his new territory. For a dog that appeared out of a cornfield, he was making himself at home in the suburbs.

Way faster than I had.

I couldn't wait for Ellison, Roger, and Ruthie to meet him. But that would have to wait until morning. It was late, and Dad would be leaving soon. Time to say goodbye, as usual. And to get Arrow fed and settled in the house.

Up in my bedroom, Midge and I set up the cardboard doghouse. On the bottom, we spread out a couple of the towels Dad used to wash the car.

Arrow sniffed at his new bed, slimed one of the yogurt-lid windows with his wet nose, and stepped inside. He scratched at the towels, turned in three circles, and plopped down.

Midge slid a small note through the mail slot.

He sniffed it.

I picked up the note and read it to him.

Deer Tyrannocanis rex Arrow,

Welcom to Cherry Avenue. We love you!!!

Midge and Jack

P.S. Pleeez don't join the circus agin. Or go in the cemetary.

I refolded the note and set it back into the box. "Why not go into the cemetery?"

Midge softly howled, "*Owoooooo!*"

Arrow's eyes were closed, but his ears twitched.

Then Midge held her curled index fingers up to her mouth like sharp teeth.

How could I have forgotten about the coyote? Arrow definitely wasn't a match for a wild animal with fangs. "Don't worry. I'll protect him."

Midge sat with her knees pulled up under her chin. "But you can't hurt the coyote either. God made him too."

I sighed. It's impossible to argue with a biologist.

Midge sniffed and wiped her nose on her left knee. Tears were hanging on to her eyelashes for dear life. (Midge does not like to cry.)

"What's wrong?"

Her voice was wobbly. "What if we can't keep him? What if his owner is a mean kid like Buzz Rubuts?"

"Ru*blatz*," I corrected. I hadn't thought of that either.

"Can we pray the dog finds a good home?"

I reached for Midge's hand. "Close your eyes . . . Jesus, please help Arrow—"

"Tyrannocanis rex."

"Please help Arrow Tyrannocanis rex find a good home. Preferably a small blue house in the suburbs with a big yard. We love him. Amen."

The growl woke me.

Was that Arrow? Or had I only dreamed I found a shaggy mutt with circus abilities and definitely no fleas?

Nope, there it was again—a low, deep growl came from the window seat beside my bed.

"Arrow?" I mumbled. I rubbed my eyes.

In the dim streetlight coming through the window, I could see Arrow's fuzzy outline, facing the window.

"Hey, boy, what's up?" I crept out of bed and crawled next to him on the seat. I put my hand on his back. His whole body was tense and shaking.

Rain had splattered the window and blurred my view.

I slid down the top sash of the narrow window so I could see better.

A light drizzle fell like glitter beneath the streetlamp at the corner of Cherry and Oak.

I pressed my nose to the screen.

Arrow did too.

I tasted rain and smelled the end of summer.

Arrow smelled something too and snorted. He growled again.

I squinted into the darkness. The streetlamp reflected off the wet streets and sidewalks.

A gray shadow came from the direction of the cemetery.

The coyote! It trotted down the sidewalk just below my window. Sparkles of light caught in its wet fur.

Arrow went into full guard dog mode, barking and scrabbling at the bottom window pane.

The coyote bolted and disappeared up Cherry and toward the woods.

He kept barking and shoving his nose against the screen.

I grabbed him, afraid he'd push right through. And wake Mom up.

Too late . . . I heard her call from the bottom of the stairs.

I slid the window back up and scrambled into bed, pulling Arrow with me.

A few seconds later I heard Mom close Midge's bedroom door. Then from my doorway, she said, "Jack, what's the ruckus?"

She shuffled into the bedroom and sat on the edge of the bed. "Why are you two up?" She yawned.

I didn't want to worry her about the coyote. But I wanted to give her a good reason for Arrow waking her up in the middle of the night. "Arrow heard something. Isn't he a great watchdog?"

Whining, he stepped over to my mom.

She scratched him under the chin. "He's a great alarm clock, anyway. Can you reset him for 8:00 a.m.?"

"Sorry. I'll try."

Mom stood up and kissed the top of my head. "Get some sleep. Both of you." She walked to the door and stopped.

I could barely see her, but I was glad she was there.

"I'm praying Arrow finds his rightful owner. And I hope it's you."

"Thanks, Mom."

I snuggled back under my sheet and pulled Arrow to my chest. His body was still kinda tense. His heart was thumping even faster than mine. I figured Mom wouldn't mind if he slept in my bed just this once. Maybe it would only be just this once.

"Goodnight, Arrow. Don't worry. I'll take care of you. I'll protect you from, from . . ." I didn't know what to call the coyote, but I felt like it needed a name. But I was too tired to think about it.

Instead, I fell asleep to the ups and downs of my dog's soft breaths.

9

TOP SECRET SURPRISE

Monday morning means weekly Tree Street Kids meetings in Da Bomb Shelter. That's Ellison's name for our fort. I mapped the layout and what we still needed to outfit it.

Today's meeting agenda was packed:

1. Top secret surprise
2. Ruthie: photo of the week
3. Roger: how-to for the week—slingshots
4. Ellison's book report and special invite
5. Midge's nature report

Midge and I headed to Mr. Bruno's early. Mr. Bruno had given me my first lawn-mowing job in the neighborhood.

That's how I discovered what was hiding under the ground. And that's why we have an old bomb shelter for a fort.

Mr. Bruno was already banging and clanging in his garage. Dressed in his usual denim overalls and white undershirt, he was hard at work on something greasy. And probably from the 1940s.

Arrow loved him as soon as he sniffed the back of Mr. Bruno's knotty hand.

Mr. Bruno reached into his overalls pocket and pulled out a half piece of crispy bacon. "Snack for later, but I'm glad to share."

Genius. Why hadn't I ever thought of pocket bacon?

Mr. Bruno held the bacon over Arrow's head. "Sit," he commanded.

Arrow sat.

"Beg."

Arrow stood on his back legs and pawed at the air with his front paws.

"Staaayyy . . ."

Arrow didn't blink or lick his chops, even when Mr. Bruno set the piece of bacon right on the end of Arrow's snout.

"Good boy!" Mr. Bruno slapped his leg and laughed.

Arrow shook the bacon loose and gobbled it off the floor. He jumped up, pressed his front paws onto Mr. Bruno's knees, and let him scratch him hard behind the ears.

Mr. Bruno walked with us out to the underground shelter. I lifted the round lid to the concrete shaft that led down into the ground. Dad had installed a new cover over the opening that was lighter and easier to lift than the old one. No one in the 1990s was worried about a war with Russia like they'd been in the 1960s. That's when the shelter was built by the people who used to own Mr. Bruno's house. I was glad all we had to worry about now was keeping the rain out.

The three of us stood next to the opened shaft.

Arrow sat at my feet and peeked down the ten metal steps that spiraled down into the hole. Then he looked up at me.

The sticky-outy fur over his brown eyes raised like cartoon eyebrows. *You want me to go down there?*

"For an escaped circus performer, you seem pretty iffy about a winding staircase into the ground," I said to him.

"Try this." Mr. Bruno reached into his shirt pocket again and slipped a piece of bacon into my hand.

Time to practice fetch.

I held the bacon to Arrow's nose. Then I tossed it down the shaft. It landed on the bottom step. "Fetch, boy!"

He looked up at me again and panted, which really looked like he was sticking his tongue out.

"Fine, I'll go first." I sat at the edge of the round opening and put my foot onto the first step. I wound my way down and stopped halfway, looking up.

Arrow, Midge, and Mr. Bruno all peered down at me.

"See? Easy." I patted the metal step above me. "Your turn. Bacon awaits!"

He lay down in the grass and whimpered.

"I bet he's great on the trapeze," Midge said, patting Arrow's head.

The gang would be here any minute, and I wanted to surprise them. I climbed back up, held him over my shoulder like a baby, and carefully made my way all the way down the steps.

Midge followed, talking him up like she was a circus ringmaster. "And now for his next trick, the amazing, the fuzzy, the maybe-he'll-be-braver-tomorrow T. rex Arrow will descend into the depths of the earth!"

I set him down on the concrete landing at the bottom of the staircase.

He snatched the piece of bacon from the bottom step and gobbled it down.

"We definitely have to work on your fetching skills," I said.

"And then his jumping-through-fiery-hoops circus skills," Midge added.

I pushed open the arched metal door that led into the main shelter. It was a dome-shaped room about the size of my small attic bedroom. Inside, we flicked on the two camping lanterns. They sat on the round table in the middle of the shelter. The lanterns and the morning light shining down the shaft was enough to see by.

My dad had made the table out of three pieces of wood he was able to fit down the shaft. Upside-down five-gallon buckets worked as seats. I wondered if King Arthur had started out this way.

"Have a good meeting," Mr. Bruno called down. "I'll whip up my special tuna-and-pickle sandwiches in about an hour."

"Thanks, Mr. B!" I hollered back.

Arrow sniffed all around the perimeter of the round room.

I patted the bucket that sat between my seat and Roger's.

Arrow hopped right up.

"Wow," Midge said. "Let's see if he can balance a beach ball on his nose like a sea lion." She leaned close to his face. "Hmmm, except a dog can't change its whisker asymmetry like a sea lion."

"Whisker what?"

"It's how sea lions move their long whiskers to balance beach balls."

MIDGE'S PHENOMENAL FACTS!

California sea lions have thirty-eight whiskers on each side of their face, and the whiskers can grow up to 7.5 inches. They are controlled by many small muscles (kind of like human hands), which are very sensitive to touch and water flow.[6]

"Well, I bet a sea lion can't fetch," I said. Not that Arrow was an expert. Not yet anyway.

His ears twitched, and he looked at the open door.

Ten seconds later, footsteps clanged on the steps.

Who needed sea lion whiskers with ears like that? I grabbed Arrow's collar to steady him.

As I'd planned, Midge blocked the doorway, making a small X with her arms and legs. "Halt! Everyone close your eyes for the top secret surprise! It's on the agenda," she added.

Ellison, Roger, and Ruthie craned their necks, trying to see inside the room.

"Is it a bookshelf?" Ellison asked.

"I don't really like surprises," Ruthie said.

"I'm ready for whatever it is." Roger patted the backpack full of supplies he never went anywhere without. Just like the walkie-talkie hooked to his belt.

"Rarf, rarf!"

"Whoa, a dog!" Roger said.

Everyone pushed past Midge, her twiggy appendages no match for my excited friends.

"Well, that was anticlimactic," she huffed.

Arrow jumped down from the overturned bucket and bounced from one person to the next, accepting scratches behind the ears from Ellison and hand-paw shakes from Roger.

Ruthie, a "cat person," wiped her hand on her shorts after Arrow licked it. But she snapped some pictures of the welcome with the camera that was always hanging from a black strap around her neck. *Click-clack*-flash, *click-clack*-flash, *click-clack*-flash.

Roger dropped his backpack on the table and fished out some peanut-butter power snacks his mom always made. He tossed one up in the air. Sure enough, Arrow leaped up and caught it before it hit the ground.

"You can always trust a dog that likes peanut butter," Ellison said in his book-quotey voice.

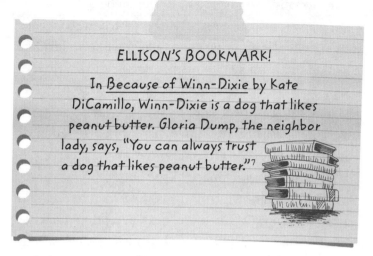

ELLISON'S BOOKMARK!

In <u>Because of Winn-Dixie</u> by Kate DiCamillo, Winn-Dixie is a dog that likes peanut butter. Gloria Dump, the neighbor lady, says, "You can always trust a dog that likes peanut butter."[7]

"This meeting will now come to order." I blew hard into the sticky, green apple whistle pop we used to start our meetings.

We all sat straight on our assigned buckets, and Arrow curled up at my feet. I guess he was pooped from all the excitement. I gave my report about how we found the dog. Plus, the bad news that he might only be a member of the Tree Street Kids for a few days.

Everyone clapped when I finished. And Ellison even gave my report an awesome title: "The Miraculous Tale of the Stray Arrow."

10

BEANS AND FANGS

Ruthie's photo of the week report was next. She's a photographer but wears an eye patch. She said it's because her right eye is kind of lazy.[8] The doctor said she has to wear a patch over her good eye to force the weak one to get stronger. Ruthie says focusing her camera is great exercise. Like lifting weights, except with your eyeball.

Ruthie laid out her newest photos on the table like a game of Memory. Her ginger cat named Captain Beans was in every single one. Capt. Beans was dressed up in costumes Ruthie and her grandma had sewn.

Capt. Beans wearing a pink tutu.

Capt. Beans with a lion's mane made from yarn.

Capt. Beans as a sunflower.

Capt. Beans dressed like a pirate. In that one, she and Ruthie were both wearing skull-and-crossbones eye patches.

I'm obviously a dog person, but I had to admit Capt. Beans really did look like she could sail the seven seas. Even if she didn't seem happy about it.

We all clapped at the end of Ruthie's report. But we sure didn't expect her to start crying.

"I think Beans is . . . is . . . sick!" She sniffed, lifting her eye patch a little to wipe her good eye. "She's getting all fat and grumpy and doesn't want to wear her tutu." Ruthie held up the picture of Capt. Beans the ballerina.

Not that the tutu fit around her big belly, I thought.

"Maybe your dad should take her to the vet," Roger suggested.

Ruthie shook her head. "He said we don't have money for that."

"Why is her name Capt. Beans, anyway?" Midge asked.

Ruthie told us that a couple years ago her mom brought the ginger kitten home in a shipping box for coffee beans. The box had a logo with an old-time ship on it. Ruthie's mom said, "Why don't you call her Capt. Beans?" So Ruthie did. And the next day her mom went away, and she hasn't been back home since.

We were all really quiet after Ruthie finished her report.

"Why didn't she come home?" Midge whispered. "Is she lost?"

Ruthie shrugged. She sniffed again and carefully gathered up her photos.

"Maybe we could take up a collection, like at church," Ellison said. He pulled a neatly folded dollar bill out of his pocket and put it on the table. "I have a dollar."

Roger scrounged around in his backpack. He retrieved a quarter and two pennies.

Midge set a chocolate-covered caramel candy on top of the small but growing pile. "Chocolate always makes me feel better."

All I had in my pockets was lint and a LEGO head. I set the smiling head on Roger's quarter. "It's like an I.O.U. I'll donate as soon as I get paid for mowing lawns."

Ruthie smiled. "Thanks, you guys."

Roger was next with his how-to. He pulled one of his homemade weapons out of his military-issue backpack. Roger wouldn't hurt a fly, but he was always prepared. "It's a slingshot."

The slingshot was an upside-down wire hanger, the triangle part squashed flat and the whole thing bent into a V shape with the hanger hook at the bottom. He'd attached the end of two long rubber bands to the top ends of the V. The other ends of the rubber bands met in the middle and were attached to a scrap of cloth.

"I'll demonstrate." Roger held the slingshot in one hand

and a bag of fruit snacks in the other. "Who wants to be my target?"

We all stood at different spots in the shelter as Roger shot fruit snacks at us. We tried to catch the fruit snacks in our mouth. A couple stuck to the wall, and a cherry one hit Ruthie in her unpatched eye. Ellison *almost* caught three in a row. But Arrow jumped in front of him on the third launch and snatched the snack in midair.

We all cheered.

Now to get that dog to actually *fetch*. I'd have to ask Ellison if he had any books on dog training.

Ellison's family basically lives in a library. The living room walls are covered with bookshelves. Books are stacked on tables and next to chairs. And the family reads instead of watching TV, which they don't have anyway. His dad works for a book publisher in Chicago, and his mom is an English professor. So Ellison reads. *A lot*. And he gives a book report every Monday. (He's gonna come in real handy when school starts.)

Today he had a book report and special invite.

He held up a paperback with a painting of a Siberian Husky—or maybe it was a wolf—on the cover.

I don't read, except for school, but a dog book might be cool.

"This book is about a dog that's part wolf." Ellison switched on his dramatic book voice that always made him sound at least twelve. "*White Fang*, feared by everyone, loved by no one."[9]

"That sounds sad," Midge protested. She hurried over to Arrow, who was curled up at my feet again and covered his ears. "I would love White Fang."

"Not if he woke you up in the middle of the night," I said.

That's when it hit me. I had the perfect name for our sneaky, toothy, wild coyote . . .

FANG.

11

SUPER STEWARD
SURVIVAL CAMP

I would put the name "Fang" to a vote, right after Midge gave her report. I'd promised she could tell the story about our coyote adventure since I was getting to introduce Arrow.

Midge popped up from the floor. "That reminds me. I saved Jack from a coyote!"

"Hey, it's not your turn yet—wait, what do you mean *you* saved *me*?"

Midge ignored me and launched into her obviously exaggerated version of the story. "We were standing in the cemetery in the dead of night . . ."

"Whoa, 10-9, come again?"[10] Roger responded in walkie-talkie code. "You guys were in the cemetery? With a coyote?"

"Yea, his dumb yowling woke me up and freaked out Arrow." When he heard his name, Arrow sat up and wagged his tail. I grabbed a stray fruit snack off the floor and tried to balance it on his nose.

"Technically," Midge interrupted again, "it was probably a signal to let his friends know where he was."

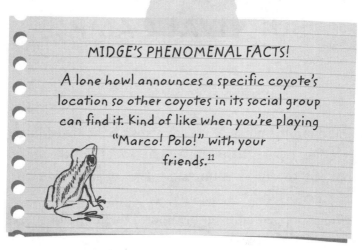

MIDGE'S PHENOMENAL FACTS!

A lone howl announces a specific coyote's location so other coyotes in its social group can find it. Kind of like when you're playing "Marco! Polo!" with your friends.[11]

"*Technically*," I said, "Midge didn't save my life."

Arrow shook his head. The fruit snack fell onto the concrete floor. He just licked it.

"I hate coyotes." Ruthie crossed her arms. Her eye was still puffy. From the crying or the fruit snack target practice, I wasn't sure. "They kill pets."

Midge stood with her fists on her hips and faced Ruthie. "It's not the coyote's fault people leave delicious-looking wiener dogs in the yard."

"I just think coyotes should stay in the woods where they belong," Ruthie said. "I always have to watch Capt. Beans when we let her outside so she doesn't become an after-school snack."

I imagined Arrow sitting on a giant cracker with a slice of cheddar cheese.

Which was worse? Worrying Arrow would end up as a cheesy coyote treat? Or knowing he might not be here to worry about?

"And if a coyote bites you, you could get rabies," Ruthie argued.

I wondered if she'd been talking to my mom.

"What's rabies?" Roger asked.

Midge leaned over the table and made fangs with her fingers. "It makes you grow fur on your face and go craaazzzyyy!"

"No," Roger said, slowly shaking his head, "I think that's puberty."

Ellison raised his hand like we were in school.

"Quiet down everyone." I waved my hands to shush them. "Ellison didn't finish his report."

"Actually, I have something even more exciting than a book report."

I knew that was a lot coming from someone who could pull book quotes out of his pocket as fast as I could pull lint out of mine.

This time he pulled several pieces of paper out of his back pocket, all folded into neat squares. He passed one out to each of us.

"You're all invited to my church for . . . the Super Steward Survival Caaammmppp!" He made the last word echo.

Ellison's church was where my family had been going since the Henrys first invited us after we moved to the neighborhood.

He read from the flyer. Dramatically, of course.

SUPER STEWARD SURVIVAL CAMP

(like VBS but with badges!)

Everyone Welcome!

August 14-18, 1995

For kids in K-6 grades

2nd thru 6th graders—Learn how to:

• Build a shelter •

• Start a fire with sticks •

• Be a good steward of God's earth •

Earn badges and compete against other teams
for the ultimate Super Steward badge!

Kindergarten thru 1st—
Learn nature crafts and songs about creation

And for everyone—*Games, snacks, and MORE!*

Leader: Noe Hernandez, Youth Pastor
Deer Creek Christian Church and School

"This sounds so cool!" Roger said, looking over the edge of his flyer. "What's V-B-S?"

"Vacation Bible School," Ellison said. He walked over to the cooler we kept our snacks in and grabbed five juice boxes.

"But not vacation like going to Disney World," Midge added.

Roger's eyes darted to each of us. He squirmed a little on his bucket. "Um, I think my family may be going on a camping trip that week. To Australia."

Obviously, Roger was not going camping in Australia. I figured maybe he was worried about the "Bible" part of VBS. "We need you on our team if we're gonna win the Super Steward badge," I said. "Maybe your family could go to Australia another time."

"You don't need to know about the Bible," Ellison said, handing out the juice boxes.

Roger didn't look convinced. He unwrapped his small bendy straw and stuck it into the juice box. He quietly sucked down his fruit punch.

Midge piped up. "Yeah. Jack only knows one verse. 'Jesus wept.'"

I would have been mad at her, except it actually seemed to make Roger feel better.

"Really?" Roger finished with an impressively loud slurp. "Then I'm in."

12

THE RADICAL RANGERS

A week had gone by since Arrow had found me. Any day now, Grandpa could call me to say he'd heard from Arrow's real owner. So, I wasn't crazy about being apart from Arrow for five mornings of survival camp. (He still couldn't fetch, so we'd been practicing. Once, he picked up a stick lying in the grass, but then he wouldn't let go.)

Being with the Tree Street Kids made up for not seeing him, I guess. Plus, since Roger was a church camp newbie, we all needed to be there for him.

MONDAY—HOW TO BUILD A SHELTER

A bazillion kids sat on the grass soccer field behind
Deer Creek Church and School on the first day of Super
Steward Survival Camp. Everyone had divided into grade
levels and then into teams of three to four people.

Choosing our team was easy: me, Ellison, Roger, and
Ruthie, who had decorated her eye patch with an "RR"
made out of green sequins. I guessed for Radical Rangers.

Teams fell into three categories:

> The Cunning Coyotes—second and third graders
> The Radical Rangers—fourth and fifth graders
> The Awesome Hawks—sixth graders

Hopefully, for Midge, being a Cunning Coyote made up
for not being with us.

Between the buzzing swarm of kids and the back entrance of the school, a small, low stage was set up. Soon-
to-be seventh- and eighth-grade helpers nearly overflowed
the edges. They all wore bright blue T-shirts with the yellow camp logo—the earth with the words, "In his hand is
the life of every creature (Job 12:10)." All us kids got yellow
T-shirts with a blue camp logo.

I was eager to get to the survival stuff. I figured learning
some skills might come in handy protecting my territory
from Fang and . . .

. . . a snarling voice snuck up behind me. Its hot breath raised chills on the back of my neck. "You *better* learn some survival skills. You're gonna need 'em."

I froze like a bullfrog in the beam of a flashlight. It could only be . . .

. . . Buzz Rublatz.

What was he doing here? Then I remembered the flyer Ellison had handed out to all of us. It said: Everyone welcome!

Coyotes in the suburbs, and now this.

A real-live hulk holding a Bible squeezed himself onto the front of the stage packed with cheerful camp volunteers. "Welcome Super Stewards!" his voice blared through the microphone.

Buzz huffed and backed away at the announcement. But his hot dog and onion breath hung menacingly in the air. (Who eats hot dogs for breakfast anyway?)

Phew! Nothing like a man with a booming voice and a Bible to save the day.

The man adjusted the microphone but didn't really have to—he wasn't much taller than the seventh- and eighth-grade volunteers surrounding him. But his arms were big enough to lift the stage—and everyone on it—right over his head and spin it on one finger.

"I'm Noe—"

His voice was a sonic boom. It would have knocked us down, except we were already sitting.

The microphone screeched the last part of his name: No-*eeeeee!*

Kids clapped their hands over their ears.

"Oops, sorry about that," he said, moving back a step. "I'm Noe Hernandez, the youth pastor here at Deer Creek."

Noe didn't look like the kind of guy who said "oops." The earth logo on his camp T-shirt stretched into an egg shape across his huge chest. He had a black crew cut and a thorn tattoo around a bicep that was as big as my head.

He didn't look like a pastor. He *did* look like he could crush cars with his bare hands.

Ellison elbowed my right arm. "I told you my youth group leader was cool."

Noe said we could call him by his first name, which I'd never done with a grown-up without putting a Mr. or Miss in front of it.

Noe explained what we'd be learning this week: cool facts about nature, basic survival skills, and ways we could be good stewards of the earth because . . .

"God put people in the garden of Eden to 'work it and take care of it,'" he said, pointing at across the sea of bed-heads. "That means every single one of you. No skips."

He flipped open his Bible. It hung over his palm like a bird in flight. "Do you know that you can see God all around you, like in the faces of your friends?"

Heads swiveled back and forth.

I looked at Ellison and smiled.

He smiled back at me and proudly swept his hand over the side of his flattop haircut.

I turned to my left. Ruthie and Roger were making crazy faces at each other.

"Look up."

Everyone looked up.

The sky was a sky blue crayon, and sun fried my right cheek like an egg.

"Listen."

Birds chirped. A breeze rustled the leaves in the trees behind us.

"Smell."

Besides my clothes still smelling like pancakes, the air smelled kind of watermelony. And like grass and fabric softener and sweaty kids.

"You want to see God? You want to know who He is?" Noe asked.

His voice was starting to boom again, so he stepped down from the stage and started to walk through the crowd of kids. We parted like the Red Sea before Moses. "This is what it says in the book of Job.

> "*But ask the animals, and they will teach you,*
> *or the birds in the sky, and they will tell you;*

or speak to the earth, and it will teach you,
      or let the fish in the sea inform you.
Which of all these does not know
      that the hand of the LORD *has done this?*
In his hand is the life of every creature
      and the breath of all mankind."

Noe swept his arm wide. "We are all part of this amazing creation. Yet, God has also made us the stewards, caretakers." He pointed to the second and third graders sitting in the front: "The Cunning Coyotes!"

I saw Midge's blond head thrown back as she let loose her best coyote impression. The other second and third graders howled along with her. *Yip, yap, yeeeooow!*

Noe pointed at the fourth and fifth graders. "The Radical Rangers, man!"

We whooped, clapped, and shrugged. No one was sure what sound a ranger actually made.

He pointed at the sixth graders behind us. "And the Awesome Hawks!"

Even though they were the smallest group, their screeching sent chills down my arms. My friends glanced behind us. But I didn't want to see Buzz lock eyes on me like a bird of prey on a limping mouse.

Ellison leaned closer. "Guess they're our competition for the Super Steward badge," he said.

Fine with me. I was ready. At least I would be after snack time.

"This isn't only about learning to care for God's earth," Noe said. "You are going to learn some legit survival skills, like building a shelter."

He trotted back to the stage, stood behind the mic, and closed his Bible. "And at the end of the week, you'll all put what you learned to the test in the Super Steward Survival of the Fittest-Legitest-Not-Gonna-Quittest Scavenger Hunt!"

Howls, screeches, and random ranger noises drowned out the volunteers now breaking into a sing-along with lots of hand motions I didn't know. Except the one for all of us to stand up and join in.

Ellison was basically busting a move.

Ruthie was grabbing action shots of the chaos.

And Roger was reaching for his walkie-talkie. His mom (aka Mothership in walkie-talkie code) had allowed him to turn it off during camp. He looked ready to call in a 10-16 for her to come pick him up. For a kid who had an Army-issued backpack covered in merit badges, like home dentistry and wound care, he didn't seem very prepared for a few hours of church camp. I guess this was uncharted territory.

I stood awkwardly until the music stopped.

As the crowd clapped, Ruthie held her camera out at

arm's length. "C'mon, c'mon, squish together." She aimed
the lens at all four of us, and said, "Say, radical!"

"Radical!"

Click-clack.

13

HOW TO BUILD
A SHELTER

While the Cunning Coyotes headed into the church building for craft time, the Rangers and Hawks learned the first rule of survival: if you ever get lost in the woods, S.T.O.P.P.

Volunteers held up poster boards with each letter painted in a different color. Each volunteer shouted out the rules in order, and then explained them.

"**S** is for stop or sit down!"

Panicking makes things worse and keeps you from making good decisions.

"**T** for think!"

How did you get where you are? Could you retrace your steps? What do you need and what do you have with you that might be useful?

"**O** for observe!"

Look around you. What's the weather like? What time might it be depending on where the sun is in the sky? What things are in the area that might help you stay safe?

"**P** for plan!"

Depending on the situation, one of the first things to decide is whether to stay where you are or to keep moving.

The last volunteer shouted, "**P** is for pray!" and held up the final letter.

Ask God for protection, help, and guidance.

Next to me, Roger furiously scribbled notes in his small, green military tactical notebook. It looked like he was getting the hang of VBS.

The Tree Street Kids were going to be prepared for anything.

We broke into our teams and headed to the back end of the grassy field, like excited swarms of bees. It was time to build a shelter and earn our first badge.

Twelve big piles of branches were arranged in a wide circle.

Noe, along with two volunteers, stood in the middle of the circle next to another pile of branches. "Each team choose a pile!" he boomed through a megaphone.

Everyone scattered.

Buzz made sure his team ended up right next to ours. He even chased away the other team that had already claimed the spot first. But you didn't argue with a sixth grader who said, "Beat it!" like he might eat you for lunch.

"Shelter is priority number one when you're trying to survive in the woods," Noe said. "Now our camp volunteers Ashley and Darnell are going to show you how to start building an A-frame shelter."

Noe explained we could only use our own pile of branches and anything in our camp knapsacks. The drawstring knapsacks matched our yellow T-shirts with the blue earth logo.

"Solid construction counts," Noe said, "*but*, so does speed. Let's pretend the sun is setting soon, and you hear thunder rumbling in the distance. You have one hour before it turns dark and the rain hits. GO!"

The teams scrambled, some kids laughing and chatting, others shouting and barking orders—namely Buzz. Volunteers walked around the circle. I guess to watch our progress. And hopefully to make sure Buzz didn't cheat.

The four of us scurried around our pile of branches.

"Stop!" Ellison said.

We halted and stared at him.

"S for stop," he reminded us.

"T for think," Roger said. He wore his camp knapsack

over his Army backpack. Roger shrugged both packs onto the ground. He emptied the yellow knapsack into the grass. "How can we use what we have in new ways?"

My brain took inventory:

> A glow stick
> A bottle of water
> A couple wide rubber bands, like the kind the grocery store wraps around broccoli (I felt sorry for the person who had to eat all that broccoli to get enough rubber bands for a hundred kids.)
> Five granola bars, one for each day of camp
> A bright yellow rain poncho

The bag lay crumpled to the side.

I glanced around the field at the other teams. Most of them were having a hard time keeping the long top branch from falling off the support branches stuck into the ground at both ends of the shelter.

"Jack, take off your knapsack and empty it," Roger ordered. "We can use the shoulder strap cords to tie the ends of the top branch to the supports."

I dumped my pack, and we both went to work securing the ends of the long branch to the two support branches.

"O—observe. Remember, like Noe said, pretend we're in the deep woods and a storm is coming," Ruthie said.

She raised her camera and scanned the sky. "I spy dark clouds and lightning on the horizon. And I hear thunder and smell rain coming." She swung her camera back toward us. "If we were in the woods, I'd make sure there's no dead branches hanging over our heads that might fall and squash us. Also, Jack, you have a leaf stuck in your hair. Smile everyone."

We smiled.

Click-clack.

14

P IS FOR PLAN AND . . .

And P is for plan." I studied the pile of branches. Pieces of the shelter started fitting themselves together in my head. "Ellison and I can pull out the bare branches for the slanted walls. Roger and Ruthie, you guys sort out the leafy branches. We can use them for shingles to keep out the rain and wind."

We started to dig into the pile.

"Stop!" Ellison said. "I mean for real. We forgot the last P. Pray."

"It's a pretend storm," Ruthie said. "We don't have to pray unless there's an emergency."

"Yeah, kind of like a 10-200." Roger imitated a static-y radio voice. "God needed at this location, over."

I dropped the straight, bare branch I pulled from the pile. "Ellison is right. Noe said it's the most important part." Then I surprised myself. "I'll say a prayer."

Even Ellison bugged his eyes out at me. *You?*

I guess Noe's enthusiasm was rubbing off on me.

We huddled together. I ignored the fact that the other teams were busy beating us.

Before I closed my eyes, I glanced around our tiny circle.

Ruthie was folding her hands and had her eye closed.

Roger bowed his head and tapped his gym shoe like he was keeping time to a really fast song.

Ellison peeked over his glasses and gave me a thumbs up.

"You *better* pray, Jack." Buzz Rublatz hurled his snarky comment across the invisible boundary line between our shelters. "I can build a better shelter than you can with my eyes shut."

I wondered if he could build it with his mouth shut. I also wondered how he knew my name, then I remembered we were all wearing name tags. I ignored him. "God, um, thanks for trees, and um, help us to learn stuff today and make a really good shelter." I almost added "way better than Buzz's." But, instead, I just said, "Amen."

We went back to work sorting—heavy bare branches for the walls and leafy twigs for covering. After that, we worked fast to get the shelter walls up, both sides of the A leaning against the top branch in no time. Then we worked on weaving the leafy twigs in and out of the branch walls.

I looked around the big circle. Most of other shelter walls were wonky or collapsing. I had to admit that Buzz's was pretty impressive. I elbowed Ellison and nodded toward what looked like a big cage at the end of the A-frame.

Buzz caught us looking. He pointed at me, then at the cage.

"Five minutes!" Noe roared through this megaphone. "The woods are getting dark and the rain is about to hit." Noe made an impressive attempt at a lightning sound effect.

Our pile of branches had been reduced to a few pieces of bark and twigs, one about as long as my arm with a lone green leaf.

I picked it up and wedged the end it into the knapsack cord securing the branches at the tip of the A, just above the door.

The leaf fluttered like a little green flag.

"Now it's an official Tree Street Kids shelter," I said.

"Time is up!" Noe stood in the center of the circle, ready to award the badges.

All the teams gathered around. Everyone earned a Build a Shelter badge, a yellow circle with a brown tent in the middle. One team got a bonus badge for resourcefulness. They'd used all four of their knapsacks—two the way we had, then one for a mailbox and another for a windsock to tell them which way the wind was blowing.

"And the second bonus badge goes to—"

Buzz stood next to his stick jail with his arms crossed and a smug look on this face. If he had the chance, I knew I'd be his first prisoner of war.

"Jack, Ellison, Roger and Ruthie for—"

Buzz glared at me. Forget being his prisoner, he looked at me like I was gonna be lunch.

"—remembering to S-T-O-P-P!"

We cheered and slapped Ellison on the back.

He shook his head like he was embarrassed, but he still had a big grin on his face.

Noe walked over and handed each of us a small round pin, blue with the yellow earth logo on it. Then he lifted his massive, tattooed arm and gave us each a high five. It hurt a little.

15

THE WASTED BONE

I spent the rest of the afternoon mowing lawns. And using the book Ellison lent me—*10 Easy Tricks to Teach Your Pooch*[12]—to try to teach Arrow how to fetch a stick or baseball. After a bazillion fails, I thought about throwing the book instead.

Just when I thought Arrow was chasing the ball—squirrel!—he'd swerve and go after it instead. Then come back to the ball. Chew it, slobber on it, drop it. But never bring it back to me.

Mom even gave me a raw knuckle bone to throw. "You seem to need it more than my beef soup does," she said.

I let Arrow sniff the juicy, pink bone. Right before he

could snatch it out of my hand, I yanked it away. I hurled the bone across the side yard.

It clunked against the high wooden fence and fell onto the gravel driveway.

Arrow stared toward the fence, then trotted off . . . in the opposite direction. He headed to the big maple tree behind the house and lifted his leg.

"Fine, we'll take a break," I said, walking over to him.

He looked at me and wagged his tail, like he had something to be proud of.

"But you can tell Mom she wasted a perfectly good soup bone."

We both collapsed onto the grass under the shade of the huge maple. Even though we lived on Cherry, there wasn't a single cherry tree. It would have been nice to lie in the grass with a big pile of cherries on my belly, eating them and seeing how high I could spit the pits into the air.

Instead of a pile of cherries, Arrow's head was resting on my belly.

"Maybe you should get a frog," Midge said. She was sitting on the patio, sketching in her camp nature notebook. A dead black and orange butterfly was splayed out in front of her on the concrete. She'd picked it out of the car grille— "for scientific research"—after we got home from church. "Frogs are natural non-fetchers. It'd be way less pressure on you."

Arrow raised his big eyebrows at me, and his tail thumped half-heartedly. "Don't worry. You can't be replaced," I said, making sure Midge could hear, "even by a frog that could catch fly balls. Haha, get it? *Fly* balls."

"Ha, amphibian humor," Midge said, shaking her head. "Classic."

I laid my hand on top of Arrow's bony head.

If Grandpa found Arrow's owner soon, I might end up with a frog after all. But, until then, I was determined to teach Arrow something . . . something he'd never forget. That way, he'd never forget me.

When you have a dog, you have to take him out at night. Even before you scoop a mountain of strawberry ice cream into a bowl and cover it with chocolate syrup.

And when your dad works out of town and puts you in charge of man stuff, you also have to take the garbage out at night.

I yanked the stuffed garbage bag up out of the kitchen garbage can, tied it, and lugged it out the back door.

Arrow was right on my heels. He bounded down the back steps and bounced from tree to flower to rock like a pinball. After he was done sniffing and marking his territory, he took off to the far end of the back yard.

The air was warm and still. The setting sun was turning the sky into an orange bonfire.

I dropped the garbage bag onto the narrow sidewalk that led from the patio to the garage. My chore could wait a little longer.

Instead, I chased after my dog. We ran and roughhoused until it was nearly dark.

"C'mon, boy, time to feed the garbage can."

He followed me back to the house. I grabbed the garbage bag and headed toward the garage where the garbage cans sat against the high wooden fence.

Arrow trotted along beside me. Halfway there, he halted and let out a deep growl.

Standing beside the fence, not far from the garbage cans, was Fang. The coyote froze, something clenched between his jaws.

I squinted in the fading light. Was that . . . ? No way!

Fang had fetched the soup bone.

Arrow barked a warning and ran several feet forward.

The hackles along Fang's neck bristled.

"Arrow, come!" I ordered.

Fang looked at me, drool dripping from around the round bone.

I heaved the garbage bag into the air. It landed with a crunch on the gravel driveway.

Spooked, Fang spun away from us and ran toward the street.

I lunged at Arrow, grabbing him by the scruff of the neck.

He barked one more time as Fang once again disappeared up Cherry Avenue and toward the woods.

I hugged Arrow against me, both our hearts pounding. "Next time, the soup bones stay in the soup."

16

HOW COYOTE BROUGHT FIRE

Tuesday—the second day of survival camp. All the kids gathered in the church yard again.

I held the schedule out in front of me so my team could read the sheet of paper too. Lots of activities were listed inside the border of campfire clip art. But I focused on five important words:

HOW TO BUILD A FIRE

The only thing better than learning how to build a shelter was how to build a fire.

Midge wasn't too happy to find out that the Cunning Coyotes would be learning fire *safety* instead of how to actually *build* a fire.

This was going to be great. I folded up the piece of paper and shoved it into my back pocket. "Don't worry, I'll teach you whatever I learn," I promised her before she headed off to join the rest of her pack.

The morning started with the theme song for the day, "Light the fire in my soul."[13]

Ellison pressed his palms high over his head in a candle flame formation. Ruthie and I followed his lead, waving our arms back and forth to make a flicker motion. Roger stood frozen, mostly looking like someone had blown him out.

I hadn't spied Buzz yet, and I was feeling doubtful about the wisdom of encouraging a kid like him to start a fire.

Noe hopped up on the small stage with his megaphone and introduced a special guest, his friend Hank, a real forest preserve ranger.

Hank sat on a chair on the small stage. He had a wide face, even though he didn't seem like the most smiley guy in the world, and black hair pulled back into a thin ponytail that hung just over his shoulder. His beige shirt and dark-green pants probably helped him blend right into the woods.

"Since we're learning about building fires today," Noe said, "I thought it might be fun for Hank to tell us an animal tale. Not the kind that wags, ha, ha."

Ugh. Even at church camp, I couldn't get away from coyotes.

First, Hank told us some facts about coyotes, like how they are good for land with crops because they keep down the mouse population. And even the rats in the city.

I'd never imagined coyotes living in the city. It'd been weird enough to see a coyote in the suburbs.

Hank explained that the coyotes' habitat had shrunk over the years, but that they were extremely resourceful.

"Just like you, Roger," Ruthie whispered.

Everyone was quiet as Hank's voice rumbled over our heads . . .

Once upon a time, the world was cold. The only ones who had fire were the fire sisters who lived on the mountain. And they wouldn't share fire with the people who lived at the bottom of the mountain.

Coyote saw that the people were shivering and wanted to help. So he came up with a plan.

Okay, I had to admire that. A guy's gotta have a plan.

Since the sisters always took turns guarding the fire, Coyote knew he'd have to be sneaky and quick. And he'd need help from the other animals of the forest.

One dark night, he crept close to the fire and snatched one of the burning sticks in his jaws. Then he ran as fast as he could down the mountain.

But the fire sisters chased him, coming so close their breath scorched his fur. He kept running until he couldn't run anymore. Just then, his friend Cougar appeared, and grabbed the burning stick with his sharp teeth. It was like a relay race. Now Cougar was running, and the fire sisters chased him instead. Down the mountain the animals carried the fire.

Cougar passed it to Fox.

Fox passed it to Squirrel.

Squirrel passed it to Antelope.

By then, the burning stick was only a glowing coal, so Antelope tossed the coal to Frog who swallowed it.

The fire sisters were closing in.

Frog hopped away and swam across a deep river. When he was too tired to take one more hop and the fire sisters were just about to grab him . . .

I suddenly imagined Buzz chasing Frog with his giant net.

Frog spit the coal into Wood.

The fire sisters couldn't figure out how to get the coal out of Wood, and, defeated, they retreated back to the top of the mountain.

Later, Coyote showed the cold, shivering people how they could get fire out of Wood by rubbing two sticks together, then feeding the fire with dry grass and twigs and logs. That's how coyote brought fire to the people.

The people were never cold again.[14]

The last thing I expected was to be rooting for a coyote.

But then I remembered that in real life, coyotes think puppies are snacks.

"That was an awesome story," Ellison said.

I had a feeling it wouldn't be long before he was quoting coyote tales.

I searched the crowd of Cunning Coyotes for Midge. I was betting Hank's story might make up for not getting to build her own fire. I didn't have to search long.

A few rows ahead of me, she was on her knees, face to the sky, and her blond flyaway hair lit up by the sun. She let loose a howl.

And all the other Cunning Coyotes joined in.

17

THE FIRE RACE

All the shelters were still up from the day before. Since they weren't big enough for more than one or two people at a time, we took turns sitting inside them. Each team was going to build a small fire near their shelter . . . just not too close! A jug of emergency water sat at each station.

We learned some safety tips first and how most wildfires are caused by people not putting their fires out. In some places, like the forest preserve, you can't even build a fire.

And we learned there are three ways to start a fire without matches. One is to use a fire flint, which no one had, not even Roger. The second is a magnifying glass or curved lens to focus the sunlight on something like paper . . . not so handy at night or when it's cloudy. The third, which we were about to learn, is the hardest. Radical ranger kind of stuff. We were going to use a bow and spindle.

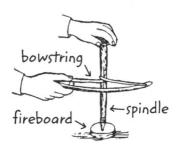

Roger, like I said, is always prepared. He already knew how to twist the bowstring around the spindle. He fit the bottom of the spindle into the notch in the fireboard. Then he pressed the hand block against the top of the spindle to hold it steady.

We took turns turning the spindle. As soon as someone's arm got tired, we switched.

After about twenty minutes, most of the teams had given up. But I was determined to get the tinder at the bottom of the spindle to light.

No coyote was going to best me. I would bring fire to my people! On my next turn, a skinny ghost of smoke rose from the fireboard.

"It's working!" Ellison burst out.

Not far off, I heard Buzz. "I'll fix *them*!" he barked at one of his teammates.

Roger put his face right next to the fireboard. He blew a long breath onto the dry grass at the bottom of the spindle.

Nothing happened, no flame. He only scared away the smoke for a second.

"Maybe the grass isn't dry enough." Ellison crouched beside me. He craned his neck and looked past me. "No one else is having much luck either."

"Not even the camp volunteers. Darnell and Ashley don't even have smoke," Ruthie reported, spying through her zoom lens.

Roger searched through his camp knapsack. "Does anyone have anything else we could use? That's VBS approved?"

"Ellison," I said, not letting up on the bow, "in my right back pocket. Camp schedule."

Ellison pulled out the folded paper. The three of them started to tear it into thin, curling strips.

Roger brushed the grass away from fireboard. He touched the tip of a strip of paper to the foot of the spindle.

A tiny spark caught. A line of orange chewed at the end of the paper. A tiny flame flickered.

I put the bow down. Ellison added the dry grass back, and Roger blew on the flame until the tinder caught too.

"WE DID IT!"

The yell of triumph came from Buzz.

I turned around to see a fire at least three times the size of ours burning at Buzz's feet.

"No. Way." Ellison said.

"So what? We can still come in second," Ruthie said. "Add the twigs!"

I just sat back on the grass, defeated. I couldn't take my eyes off Buzz. Next, he'd be roasting wienies.

"I make FIRE!" Buzz beat his chest like a caveman while his teammates high-fived. He glared at me, and a snarl tugged the lip up over his pointy canine tooth.

The sun caught on something dangling from his front pocket—a flat piece of metal hanging from a chain. A fire starter! Buzz hadn't used the bow. He'd been hiding a striker the whole time and used it to make a spark when he saw he was about to lose.

Buzz must have noticed me eyeing it because he looked down at his pocket and shoved the fire starter out of sight. He smiled at me. A big, toothy, what-are-you-gonna-do-about-it? smile.

"Yo, Jack!" Ellison poked me in the back.

When I turned back toward my team, I realized they'd managed to get a nice little fire going.

Other teams were gathering around to see Buzz's fire . . . and ours too.

I wished I hadn't wasted time worrying about Buzz.

Ruthie told Ellison and Roger to pose on either side of me. She snapped a picture of the three of us sitting behind the fire we'd built.

Click-clack. "Uh-oh," she said, zooming in on something behind us. "Looks like Noe is having a talk with Buzz. And I don't think it's about a bonus badge."

I glanced over my shoulder and saw Buzz handing his fire starter to Noe. He shoved his hands deep into his empty pockets, and his shoulders slumped. His three teammates dumped their jug of water over their fire.

"Maybe we should tell Noe about the flyer," I said to Ellison. "After all, it wasn't part of our knapsack supplies."

We voted, and everyone agreed, although Roger said we were just being resourceful.

Noe agreed when we told him. But he said *technically* we were only supposed to use the materials we were given. So no bonus badge.

But that was okay. We still earned our fire building badge like everyone else who tried.

And, *technically*, I'd beaten Buzz Rublatz.

18

GOD'S TERRITORY

On Wednesday, our teams made up plays about how our choices could hurt the environment.

Buzz had way too much fun pretending to be a chainsaw in an Amazon rain forest. Midge played the part of an endangered dragonfly. She was supposed to die dramatically when a mall was built over her wetlands habitat. Instead, she spread her arms out at her sides and flew through the audience of kids, hollering, "I'm a *Somatochlora*! You'll never catch me, urbanization!"[15]

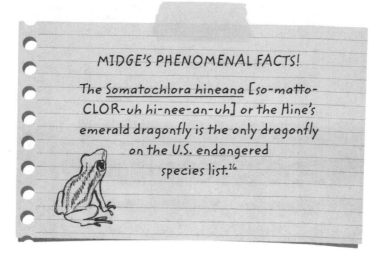

MIDGE'S PHENOMENAL FACTS!

The <u>Somatochlora hineana</u> [so-matto-
CLOR-uh hi-nee-an-uh] or the Hine's
emerald dragonfly is the only dragonfly
on the U.S. endangered
species list.[16]

I just sighed. I was ready to go home and work on my *Canis lupus familiaris*'s jumping-through-fiery-hoops circus skills.

Thursday was all about preparing for the big scavenger hunt in the forest preserve on Friday . . . and the chance to win the Super Steward badge.

Ruthie hadn't shown up for our carpool to the church that morning and no one answered the phone when Mom called.

Buzz sat smack behind me at the opening worship service inside the church.

"The woods are my territory," he said. His words swarmed around my head like yellow jackets. "I'm gonna eat the competition alive."

I caught a whiff of sweat and Old Spice, but ignored him.

At the front of the church, Noe cleared his throat.

One hundred kids shushed their jabbering.

"This is what God says in the book of Psalms . . . the best poetry you'll ever read."

I hadn't read many poems, so I took his word for it.

Noe read from the big Bible draped over his big hand. "'For every animal of the forest is mine, and the cattle on a thousand hills. I know every bird in the mountains, and the insects in the fields are mine. . . . the world is mine, and all that is in it.'"[17]

Whad'ya think of that, Buzz Rublatz? I guess the woods aren't your territory.

"What are some ways you guys care for the earth?" Noe asked.

Hands shot up all around.

Weed the garden.

Water flowers.

Mow the lawn.

Keep my cat away from baby birds.

Feed my dog.

Recycle pop cans.

Don't step on ants.

And then, from somewhere amid the sea of squeaky voices: "Save frogs from bullies!"

Uh-oh. Midge.

My back started to sweat from the heat of Buzz's glare.

"I can't wait until tomorrow," he said to whoever was sitting next to him in the pew behind us. "I'm going to win that Super Steward badge."

His voice was right behind my now sweating head. "And I don't care how many *toads* I have to smash to get it."

Before I could break sweat anywhere else, Ellison turned in his seat to face Buzz. "Man, why're you always up in Jack's grill?"

I was so used to Ellison noting key life moments in book quotes, that it took me a second to realize "up in Jack's grill" wasn't classic literature.

"Hey, we're in church, here." I lobbed the weak comeback over my shoulder.

"Yeah, we're in church," Roger said. It was kind of like adding an extra period to a sentence, but I appreciated his support.

"Even better," Buzz spit, so that I felt the "b" against the back of my head. "One, two, *three* toads to squash tomorrow."

That did it. I stood up, spun around—probably flinging nervous sweat everywhere—and leaned over the back of the pew.

Even though Buzz had pulled back out of shock, I was almost nose to nose with him. "No." I jabbed my thumb at my chest. "Just *one* toad."

Despite the fact I'd called myself a toad, I felt pretty tough, like I could take on a pack of Buzzes.

He just sat there. Smiling?

And then I realized every kid in the church was staring at me.

"Gentlemen?" Noe's big voice seemed to fill the whole church. "Is there something you'd like to add to our lesson on Psalm 50?"

Buzz stuck out his bottom lip and shook his head.

I slid back down into my seat. "No, sir. Sorry."

Noe stared at us the way my dad does when he knows for sure there's way more going on than I say.

"Good. Then, if it's all right with you, I'll explain the rules of tomorrow's scavenger hunt."

Ellison scribbled notes on being a good steward like he was prepping for a test. The rules were:

Stay with your team.
Don't leave the main trail.

Leave no trace—which means leave the woods the way you found them.

More than ever, I wanted to snag that Super Steward badge. I'd show Buzz who was top dog.

19

CAPT. BEANS IS MISSING

We need to win that scavenger hunt," I told the guys as we waited for my mom to pick us up after camp.

This called for an emergency Tree Street Kids meeting. We'd fill Ruthie in on what she missed and study up for tomorrow's hunt.

We needed a plan. A strategy. Maybe even a war cry.

The rest of the day, we needed to be laser-focused. No distractions.

"Your Grandpa called and left a message," Mom said while we were driving home. "He said for you to call him back."

So much for no distractions.

The meeting would have to wait. The call I'd been dreading had come—the call that Grandpa had found Arrow's owner.

"How did he sound?" I asked, grabbing the back of my mom's headrest. "Sad? Excited?"

"Or like the VOICE OF DOOM?" Midge said in the lowest voice she could muster.

"He sounded the way Grandpa always sounds on an answering machine," Mom said. "Like a tourist using a foreign language phrase book to ask directions to the restroom."

Ellison, sitting between me and Roger, burst out laughing. "Hahaha! Foreign language phrase book!" Then he sighed, shaking his head. "Good one, Mrs. Finch."

"Why, thank you, Ellison."

"This isn't funny," I moaned, flopping back against my seat.

"Oh, sorry," Ellison said, nudging me with his elbow. "We'll hang close while you call your Grandpa."

"Yeah, like backup." Roger leaned forward to look over at me. "We'll totally 10-23."

"He means 'stand by,'" Ellison translated.

I ran into the kitchen without taking off my shoes or knapsack and dialed our old phone number. Grandpa answered right away.

Arrow skittered across the kitchen floor, excited to see me.

I sat right down, with Arrow on my lap, and held my breath the whole time Grandpa talked.

He still sounded like he was talking to an answering machine . . . extremely uncomfortable.

Yep, someone had called the town police department about a lost dog . . . the police called Grandpa, who'd reported the lost dog . . . the man was a long-distance truck driver, just like Grandpa had thought. The man was going to be in town again this weekend. He wanted to see if the dog—the dog that had come flying like an arrow out of the cornfield and *thwack* into my heart—was his dog . . . not mine, but his.

Grandpa's voice turned softer. He said he understood how hard this was for me. "But I'm sure Mr. Davis will be glad to have his copilot back. Remember nothing belongs to us, Jack. All these wonderful creatures are the Lord's."

I could only nod, which of course he couldn't see.

"He chose you to take care of that pup. I'm sorry it wasn't for longer. I'd had Hutch for nearly twenty years. Twenty years or twenty days, either way, it can be hard to say goodbye."

Grandpa said Mr. Davis would be by Saturday. He told me he loved me. "Thanks, love you too" was all I could get out. I pushed the off button on the phone.

Ellison, Roger, Mom, and Midge were standing by.

(Well, Mom was also making us peanut butter and strawberry jam sandwiches.)

"This weekend," I mumbled. "A man is coming this weekend to see . . . the dog." I swallowed hard and put my face against Arrow's. I was glad when he licked the tears off before anyone saw them.

The phone was still in my hand when it rang again.

Arrow barked and jumped off my lap.

Ruthie's voice screeched through the receiver. I hopped up and held it away from my ear then out to Ellison.

As he listened, his eyebrows drew together the way they do when he's reading a book and comes to a tense scene. "Oh, no. Okay. Sure. We were about to call an emergency meeting anyway. We'll meet you at the shelter."

Ellison glanced sideways at Midge. She was at the kitchen table stuffing her camp knapsack with snack-sized bags of cheddar cheese goldfish-shaped crackers.

He lowered his voice. "Yeah, just the four of us can meet."

We all looked at Midge to make sure she hadn't heard him.

She flashed a big smile.

We all smiled back.

Ellison hung up and set the phone on the counter.

Midge narrowed her eyes at us.

I stretched my arms up over my head to block her view of my face. "What's up?" I whispered at Ellison.

Arrow wagged his tail like he was waiting to hear the news too.

Ellison motioned toward the back door with a nod of his head.

The three of us, with Arrow on our heels, nonchalantly rushed toward the back door.

Mom handed Ellison a paper bag full of sandwiches as he moved through the doorway.

Outside, Ellison blurted. "It's Capt. Beans. She's missing. Ruthie is afraid the coyote will get her. If he hasn't snatched her already."

I imagined finding Capt. Beans's tutu in a coyote den.

"Let's get to the shelter," I said. I scooped Arrow up into my arms. At least for today, nothing was going to take him from me. "Forget the scavenger hunt for now. We're gonna find Capt. Beans. This has officially become a rescue mission . . . and a coyote hunt."

20

THE EMERGENCY MEETING

In the shelter, the four of us took our regular places around the table. The guys and I dropped our knapsacks onto the table.

Arrow jumped up onto Midge's seat. This meeting was for big kids—and dogs—only.

Ruthie's eye was red and puffy from crying. I figured the other eye must be too. Over her eye patch, she'd taped a cutout photo of Capt. Beans's face. She told us Beans had disappeared early that morning. That's why Ruthie hadn't shown up for the car ride to church.

A plan was forming in my head. Each of us had skills. Maybe not fire building or hunting skills, but other skills. Now to pool our resources and figure out how to save Ruthie's pet. If she could be saved. (I decided not to mention that last part.)

Title: The Hunt for Fang (thanks to Ellison)
Mission: Locate Fang, rescue Capt. Beans, protect Arrow
Team members: Jack, Ellison, Roger, and Ruthie
(aka Tree Street Kids, aka Radical Rangers)

"Roger, you are Weapons Master," I said.

"Roger," said Roger, saluting. He plunked his Army backpack next to his knapsack. He rifled through it and pulled out his supply of homemade gadgets, laying each one on the table. "Pencil crossbow . . . ruler bow and arrow . . . clothespin peg shooter . . ."

Let's see. Book quotes wouldn't come in handy in this situation. But he did know the main trails pretty well. "Ellison?"

Ellison sat up straighter in his chair and got that bookish gleam in his eye. "They swung out upon the trail and into the silence, the darkness, and the cold."[18]

"Super impressive," I said, "but how about you be the Trailblazer?"

He responded with a silent *yesss!* and a fist pump.

I looked at Ruthie. Her eye was still full of tears. "Do you want to be—"

"I'll be *vengeance*," she growled.

"Uhhh, okay, or you can be our *National Geographic* photographer and take the official photo once we catch Fang. You know, like when a fisherman catches a shark and hangs it by the tail. Then stands next to it like this . . ."

I stood up, punched my hands onto my hips, and looked off into the fake distance.

"How exactly are we gonna *catch* it?" Roger asked.

"Yeah, it'll be pretty mad after getting dinged with rocks and shot with crossbow chopsticks," Ellison added. "Maybe we could catch it in a cage."

"And then radio for backup. 10-67, all units," Roger said. "My mom would be there in a flash."

"And then call the zoo," Ellison went on.

I sat back down and scratched my head. *Hmm*. I'd only thought of hunting the coyote. Not actually catching it.

Ruthie jumped up from her seat and slapped the photo of Ballerina Beans onto the tabletop. "Why do you need a cage? Fang is a m-m-monster!" She pointed at the photo. "He probably *ate* Capt. Beans." Then she pointed at Arrow. "Do you want your dog to be dessert?"

Arrow perked up his ears.

I shook my head. Not just to say no but to shake off the

image of Arrow sitting like a cherry on top of a giant ice cream sundae.

"Aren't you going to kill the coyote?" Ruthie asked, looking right at me. "Capt. Beans was a present from my mom."

And now she was gone. (Ruthie's cat *and* her mom.) That would make me sad too. And mad.

Ellison cleared his throat. "Technically, you can't kill anything in a forest preserve. Except maybe a mosquito."

Apparently the rest of us weren't concerned with the rules. Instead, Roger very ceremoniously passed out the weapons.

Ruthie tested the aim of her school ruler bow and arrow. She nocked the pencil missile, then she stared down the length of the sharpened No. 2 with her uncovered eye—it looked angry.

My weapon was a crossbow made out of taped-together pencils and rubber bands.

"Hey, Jack," he said, "if I'm weapons master, Ellison is the trailblazer, and Ruthie is vengeance, what're you gonna be?"

I aimed the small crossbow at the opposite wall. Solid construction. Good rubber band action. Wooden chopstick for ammo. But against a wild animal . . . ?

I gulped. "I'm gonna be toast."

21

THE HUNT BEGINS

A *tink* sounded on the metal spiral staircase. *"Shhh!"* I waved my hands in front of me.

During meetings, we never closed the shelter's hatch or main door unless it was raining.

Everyone hushed, staring at me for a good ten seconds. Maybe I was hearing things. "Nevermind. Listen, we need to replenish our supplies, grab our bikes, and head to the woods. We have to find Beans before it gets dark."

"And Fang," Ruthie said, testing out the other crossbow.

"Is that an official meeting motion?" Ellison asked me.

"Sure," I said, "I motion to ride to the woods and find Beans—and Fang—before it gets dark." I still wasn't sure what we'd do once we found the coyote.

"I second the motion," Roger said, stuffing his camp knapsack into his backpack.

"All those in favor of The Hunt for Fang commencing?" Ellison raised his hand.

"AYE!" we all shouted.

We slung our knapsacks over our shoulders and marched up the spiral steps. I went last to make sure Arrow climbed up safely.

On the way, I thought I spied a cheesy goldfish cracker on the step above me. But, *crunch*, Arrow snatched it before I could be sure.

As soon as we were above ground, I scanned the yard for any sign of Midge. She'd be no help on a coyote hunt. She might even send a warning howl to Fang. Or worse, tell Mom. Nope, this was a job for Radical Rangers.

Now to find a cat in a pink tutu. And Tree Street Kids enemy number two.

We regrouped at the stop sign at the corner of Cherry and Maple. Ruthie had changed into her yellow camp T-shirt and brought her Radical Rangers knapsack.

Roger's hanger slingshot dangled from his belt loop.

And Ellison wore a Chicago Bulls bucket hat. "It's the best safari guide hat I could find," he said, shrugging.

"This is a hunt," Ruthie said. "We're not bird watching."

Her vengeance was starting to make her grumpy.

I had my camp supplies and a full water bottle. And I had Arrow on Hutch's clothesline leash.

From behind us, I heard a grating T. rex roar—Midge's bike horn.

I twisted around just as she flew up on us, jamming on her brakes. "Hey, where are you guys going?"

Arrow trotted over to her, dragging his leash, and put his front paws up on her leg for a scratch behind the ears.

"Just for a ride on the trails," I said. "You can't come."

She wrinkled her nose at me.

"Next time, okay, Midge?" Ellison offered, trying to smooth things over. "We're going to show Jack the trails. Then he can show you." He patted my shoulder. "Right, Jack?"

"Yeah, right." I nodded and smiled really big.

Midge squinted her eyes and cocked her head. As usual, she was wearing her ladybug rain boots and the green bike helmet. It slid sideways. "Why do you all have your knapsacks?" She had hers too.

"Supplies," Roger said. Roger was all about supplies. Nothing out of the ordinary there.

"Why does Ruthie's eye look like it was crying?"

"Allergies."

"Why does Roger have his hanger slingshot?"

"Target practice."

"Why is Ellison wearing a safari hat?"

Ellison smiled smugly at us. *See?*

I sighed, looking back at Midge. "Why do you ask so many questions?

She pressed the button on her T. rex horn. It's stiff bottom jaw gaped. *Raaaaaarrrrrr!*

"Go home. Please?"

"Fine. Have fun!" She smiled, showing all her teeth.

Well, that was easy. And suspicious.

I tugged Arrow's leash and shooed Midge away. "Okay, we'll see you back at the house."

We rolled our bikes forward, checked for the usual stray car, and crossed the street.

I glanced over my shoulder. Midge still sat at the stop sign, straddling her bike. She still had that weird smile on her face. Then she waved. "Have a nice trip! Bring me a pet frog!"

The closest trail into the woods began where Cherry dead-ended at Third Street. One minute, we were cruising down Cherry toward a giant wall of green. Then, like magic, the trees parted and a dark, arched doorway opened up in front of us.

The four of us braked our bikes side by side on the gravel shoulder beside the trail entrance. The shoulder widened enough here for a few hikers to park their cars.

I stared down the trail, the end swallowed by the tunnel of old trees. The air already felt thicker when I breathed in. The musty smell stuck to the roof of my mouth.

We were about to leave behind our straight and tidy streets. (Now even tidier thanks to my lawn-mowing business.) Ellison pushed off and onto the trail.

We followed. Over our heads, past the tangle of leaves, the sky was shards of blue.

"We'll stay on the yellow trail," he said. His voice vibrated as his tires rolled over narrow ruts the rain had cut across the path. According to Ellison, all the main trails were color-coded. Thick wooden posts with a yellow circle at the top of each one stood at different spots or intersections along this trail. "The yellow trail is best for bikes," he said, "but this is no time for fun."

He was taking his Trailblazer role very seriously.

When hikers or joggers came from the other direction, Roger and Ruthie would fall behind us to clear the way.

Once in a while a side trail, just a little wider than a bike tire, snaked off the trail and disappeared into the knee-high weeds and tangled honeysuckle trees.

"What's down there?" I asked when we passed another one.

"I don't know. I've only seen hikers and forest preserve rangers go that way," he said, pedaling alongside me. "My parents said those trails are off limits until I'm twelve."

Ellison said he read that there over sixteen thousand acres of forest preserve just around our suburb and *seventy* thousand in Chicagoland.

He was starting to sound like Midge.

"It's easy to get lost. But not, like, forever," he added.

I was used to that many acres of cornfields. Trees and wetlands were a whole other world.

The trail was busy with walkers and joggers wearing bright blue, purple, and orange jogging suits and earphones.

Ruthie started waving them down and flashing a photo of Capt. Beans. She got huffier with every shrug of the shoulder or shake of the head. An elderly couple with walking sticks and matching safari hats said they'd keep an eye out.

After about twenty minutes of pedaling, stopping, pedaling, stopping, I proposed a new plan. We parked our bikes in an abandoned stone shelter and walked. We'd cover less ground, but it would be easier to take a side trail into the woods.

"Only if we absolutely *have* to," I said. "I mean, it's not like Fang is gonna be out for a little jog on the main trail."

Just so Ellison wouldn't be disobeying his parents, I volunteered to be the one to explore the forbidden side trails.

After all, I was two months closer to twelve than Ellison was. Plus, Roger wasn't allowed to be out of walkie-talkie range.

Vengeance, however, was all up for going along if it meant finding Capt. Beans.

22

ARROW IN PERIL

We continued on foot up the trail.

From farther behind us came the jabbering of a noisy group of little girls. Maybe a Brownie troop. The group had stopped on the trail to listen to the troop leader pointing at the different trees and plants.

For a split second, I swore I spied Midge's blond head popping up out of the sea of bows, beads, and braids. But it couldn't have been Midge. For one, she couldn't go past the stop sign alone. Plus, she hadn't made any friends yet. Especially that many. And besides, she would have been on her bike and wearing the green Turtle helmet.

Arrow dropped behind me. I kept walking until the

clothesline leash tightened. He barked at the girls and wagged his tail.

"C'mon boy, it's too hot to play." I tugged and he finally followed.

The late afternoon air grew stickier. The thick ceiling of leaves held in the heat like a lid on a pot of oatmeal. I swiped my face with the collar of my camp T-shirt.

We plopped down onto a log that had fallen along the trail and took swigs from our water bottles.

Arrow panted at my feet. I poured water into my cupped hand so he could lap it up.

I wanted to be home teaching him to fetch. Frustrated, I stood up and started pacing back and forth. "Listen, guys," I stopped and faced my friends. "Coyotes usually only come out at night. And they don't jog, so I think we're wasting time searching the main trail."

Ruthie's expression froze somewhere in between crying and turning into a werewolf.

Roger's face was a red beet with a plop of tired curls on top.

Ellison nodded, sending his black-rimmed glasses slipping down his sweaty nose.

"Second, if Capt. Beans ran off into the woods, or if Fang actually did, um, *kidnap* her, we aren't going to find her—"

Ruthie's eye widened in horror.

"—on the main trail," I added quickly.

"Then where?" Ruthie huffed.

The truth was . . . I didn't know.

Ruthie bowed her head and started fiddling with the lens cap of the big camera hanging around her neck. "If Arrow disappeared, you would never give up," she said. "And he isn't even your dog."

I knew she was right about both things. But it was the second thing she said that stung.

The air suddenly felt heavier than ever.

Ellison, our faithful trailblazer, hopped up and cleared his throat as if he were about to give a speech. He pointed up the trail. "Here was neither peace, nor rest, nor a moment's safety. All was confusion and action, and every moment life and limb were in peril."[19]

ELLISON'S BOOKMARK!

Ellison probably quoted <u>Call of the Wild</u> because he understood that sometimes life isn't easy. Sometimes it's uncomfortable and tiring and sweaty, even. He knew that no matter how hopeless things seemed, they had to go on.

Arrow barked in agreement.

"Exactly!" Ruthie jumped up. "Life and paw are in peril!"

Roger scrambled up and stood next to us. He unhooked his flimsy slingshot and held it over his head. "To arms!" he shouted.

I guess what Ellison meant was that this was no time to sit like an actual bump on a log. This was a time for confusion and action! This was the hunt for Fang!

And I was the leader of the hunt.

"The wildlife steer clear of humans. That's us," I reminded everyone.

Ellison nodded. "We can stay on this trail a little longer. It heads east toward the deepest part of the woods in the whole county. If Fang is anywhere, he'll be there." He pointed ahead to where the trees closed in and the trail grew narrower and darker.

I led the way.

The gravel on the main trail crunched under our feet. Squirrels argued in angry chatters. Fewer and fewer people passed us.

Soon we passed one of the off-limits side paths. The waist-high weeds and grasses barely left room for a skinny kid let alone four coyote hunters and their canine sidekick. I wondered again where the path led.

I was dying for a breeze. But the wind only rushed over the treetops, never reaching my sweating face. Underneath the knapsack, my shirt stuck to my back. I probably smelled pretty manly.

Arrow seemed happy, at least. He sniffed each crumbling log, tall green weed, and black millipede—long and thick as my finger—inching across the path. He stopped short at every wildflower growing along the trail edge and marked his territory.

Shrubs and grasses and saplings rose beyond the boundary lines. How would we ever spot a coyote—or even a fat cat in a pink tutu—in all of that?

Maybe I wasn't cut out to lead a coyote hunt. Or even a cat rescue. Maybe I wasn't so radical or cunning or awesome, no matter how many badges I earned.

The leash yanked me—and my arm—right out of my pity party.

Arrow charged forward, barking. He strained at the end of the clothesline leash. But before I could reel him in, he backed up, shook himself, and slipped right out of Hutch's old collar.

And he was off like a shot.

23

OVER THE EDGE

A rrow!" I took off after him, looping the leash around my left forearm as I ran.

Everyone followed.

Ahead of us, and to the right of the path, Arrow halted. He stood stiffly, nose pointed at the woods.

We came to a screeching halt behind him.

A gray-brown blur weaved through the tall weeds ahead of us.

"Fang!" Ruthie yelled, pointing her finger right where I was already looking.

Then *thwip!* Arrow shot into the brush.

"No!" I yelled. I lunged into the woods, leaving behind the safe trail.

Roger and Ruthie followed, running on either side of me.

"10-14! 10-31! 10-34!"[20] Roger flung 10-codes like spitballs. Prowler alert! Crime in progress! Trouble at this station!

"Vengeance!" Ruthie cried, whipping her ruler bow and arrow out of her back pocket and raising it in front of her.

From farther behind us, Ellison hollered, "Stay on the main trail. I'm not twelve yet! Stop! S–T–O–P–P!"

But I couldn't stop. I raced on, stumbling over the soft, uneven forest floor.

The low green growth hid last fall's dead leaves, gnarly tree roots, and thorny vines. Plus, I realized, a whole world of insects and seeds and tiny animals. My gym shoes crushed everything beneath them.

Leave no trace, Noe had said. But *he* hadn't been on a rescue mission.

Right that second, I wasn't thinking about saving Capt. Beans at all. I wasn't even hunting Fang. I was trying to save my dog.

I clutched the leash, wishing camp had taught us how to lasso runaway mutts.

"Arrow, no!" I was nearly begging.

Far ahead, he hurdled fallen tree limbs. Then he'd disappear into the brush and become a mere rustle in the tall weeds.

And just a few strides in the lead—the coyote.

"Fire," ordered Roger way too soon.

Pebbles, and even a couple pencils, winged past me. "Hold your fire!" I hollered.

Thorny branches and thin twigs lashed and snapped at me as I ran past the bushes and trees. My cheek stung. A drop of warm blood trickled down, and I held my arm up in front of my face to keep from getting hit again.

Ruthie, Roger, and Ellison fell farther and farther behind.

"Arrow, stop, heel, stay!" My voice cracked. I was mad at him for running off. For not staying with me.

I couldn't see Fang anymore.

What I could see up ahead was more sky and air than I should have been seeing. The trees thinned, and the green forest floor dipped out of sight.

And, suddenly, so did Arrow. He yelped, and slid over the edge of what could only be a ravine.

My voice stuck in my throat like a wad of bubble gum. *No, no, no! How did this happen?*

I stumbled to a stop and flew forward like I was sliding into home . . . right at the spot Arrow had just been. Leaves, rocks, and twigs didn't make for a soft landing. *"Oof!"* The forest floor knocked my breath—and my confidence— right out of me. But I still belly-crawled to the very edge of what turned out to be the steep side of a deep ravine. A trickling stream snaked along the bottom.

Arrow had tumbled down about ten feet. Dead leaves and mud splotched his fur.

He looked up at me and whined. One second he was shaking; the next he was scrambling for a paw-hold.

Ellison fell to his knees beside me. Roger and Ruthie crouched on the other side.

I handed Ellison the end of the clothesline leash. "Hold this tight. I'm going to get him."

I wound the too big collar around my wrist twice.

Ellison quickly backed away from the edge until the clothesline had only a little slack.

I turned around and, feet first, I shimmied backward until my legs dangled over the side of the hill. I looked at Ellison to see if he was ready.

He sat on the ground facing me and braced his feet against a tree root that snaked up out of the ground. He wound his end of the clothesline around both wrists.

Roger and Ruthie ran over to help. They picked up the slack between Ellison and me.

"Okay, lower me down."

Roger and Ruthie fed me some rope as I slid down the steep side of the hill until I lost sight of them. Dirt and pebbles followed me. I closed my eyes and tasted musty earth.

The leash pulled tight, and the frayed collar dug into my left wrist. *Please don't break. Please don't break.*

24

HEAVE-HO CROSSBOW

Arrow whined somewhere below me.

I did my best to dig the toes of my gym shoes into the side of the hill. I spit dirt out of my mouth and called up: "Give me a couple more feet!"

The rope loosened.

I slid down a little farther. My left foot found a tree root hanging out of the dirt like the rung of a ladder. I carefully put some weight on it, and—*phew!*—it held. Thank goodness I hadn't eaten an extra pancake that morning. I let go of the leash with my right hand and reached toward Arrow.

I could almost touch the top of his head with my fingertips. I tried not to look past him. It was a long way to the bottom of the hill. If he started to roll down, the fall might kill him.

"C'mon, boy, crawl up just a few inches."

He stretched his head forward. The movement caused him to slide down a few more inches out of reach.

No!

Something poked me in the ribs as I strained to reach him. My pencil crossbow. With my free hand, I pulled it out of my back pocket. Clutching the crossbow where the pencils intersected and were duct-taped together, I stretched my arm down again. I held the longer end of the homemade weapon out toward Arrow's snout.

"Get the stick, Arrow. Grab it!" I urged, trying everything but "fetch."

Arrow raised his bushy eyebrows. He hesitated, opening his mouth only a little, like I was offering him a piece of broccoli. Finally, he stretched his neck and grabbed the end of the crossbow between his teeth.

"*Rrr*," I growled. "That's it. Get the stick."

He clenched down on it. A kind of wimpy growl sounded at the back of his throat.

"Get it, Arrow. Hold on, buddy." I pulled him up slowly.

His back feet scrambled for footing but didn't find any. Spooked, he yelped, and let go of the crossbow . . . just as I let go of it too and grabbed him by the scruff of his neck.

I dragged him up to my chest and clutched him to my

right side. My left hand felt like it was about to come off the end of my arm. How would I pull us up?

"I got him!" I hollered. But barely.

The kids grunted and heaved on the clothesline.

We didn't even budge.

"On three," Ellison yelled overhead.

I kept my foot on the root, feeling another one digging into my right knee.

"One, two, three!"

I heaved off of the root under my left shoe as my friends pulled back on the clothesline. I rose a couple feet.

Taking a guess at where it was, I lifted my right foot and planted it on the root I'd felt against my knee.

"Again!" Ellison shouted. "One, two, three!"

They heaved.

I pushed off the new root, praying it would hold too.

Up I went a couple more feet.

I dug my toes into the hillside—another heave-ho from my friends—and I finally made it back to the top.

Roger grabbed a fistful of the back of my shirt and pulled me up the rest of the way. It was good to be on horizontal ground again.

Ruthie took Arrow out of my cramped arm.

"Radical rescue rangers!" Ellison cried, jumping up and down.

Everyone gathered around me to help me stand up.

My legs were shaking like crazy. I told them how I used the crossbow to pull Arrow to safety. Once I felt like I wasn't going to throw up, I held out my arms for my dog.

Ruthie gave him a hug and handed him back. Maybe she was becoming a dog person.

Arrow's dusty body quivered against me. He smelled like wet dog and dirt.

I mumbled against his ear. "Some super steward I turned out to be."

He licked my chin half-heartedly. I think he forgave me.

Roger's walkie-talkie crackled. "Mothership to Roger, over."

Roger unhooked the unit from his belt and pressed the button. "This is Roger, go ahead, Mothership."

"What's your 20?"[21]

"Yellow trail about an hour from the Third Street trailhead. Radical Ranger Rescue in progress, over."

"Return to base, pronto. Your father has the Stratego board set up. He wants to know where you are, over."

"10-4. I'll be home by 1700 hours. Over and out."

"Roger, roger."

"Sorry, guys, I've gotta go to war. Dad's in one of his battle moods." Roger stood and clipped his radio back onto his belt.

"I need to go home too." Ruthie looked out into the

woods where Fang had disappeared. "You know," she said, "just in case Capt. Beans came back home." She carefully patted Arrow's head.

He heaved a sigh and settled down into my arms.

"I'm glad your dog is okay," she said. "I'm sorry he almost . . ."

I was glad she didn't say out loud what could have happened. "I shouldn't have brought him"—and as long as I was admitting stuff—"I don't think we're going to catch Fang," I said.

Ruthie shook her head.

"But we can look for Beans again tomorrow."

Ruthie pressed her lips together and gave a small nod.

I turned to Roger. "I'm sorry I lost your crossbow. I'll help you make another one."

Roger patted the hanger slingshot hanging from his belt again. "I've got reinforcements. Anyway, it didn't help hunt Fang. Guess I'm a lousy weapons master."

"No way! If I didn't have the crossbow, I couldn't have reached Arrow."

"10-4," he said, and smiled. Then he and Ruthie headed back toward the main trail.

Ellison helped me unwind the old collar from my throbbing wrist and slip the collar back over Arrow's head. I set him on the ground.

He gave an epic shake.

"Thanks for saving us," I said to Ellison.

He shoved his glasses up and waved a mosquito away from his shiny face. "I'm radical like that."

We slowly made our way to the trail. All around our feet were bright red mushrooms, lacy mosses, skittering spiders and beetles, and even a frog.

This time I was careful to watch where I stepped.

25

CHEESY CRACKER CLUES

Roger and Ruthie had already disappeared around the bend of the main trail by the time Ellison, Arrow, and I reached it. Soon we passed the narrow side trail we'd seen before chasing Fang into the woods.

We hadn't walked much farther when Arrow trotted ahead to the end of the long leash. He sniffed the ground and chomped down on whatever he'd found. Nose to ground, he strained forward in search of something.

We jogged to catch up. I took up the slack in the leash, as Arrow tugged forward again.

I spied a tiny and very cheesy-looking snack on the trail a foot away from the tip of his snout.

A goldfish cracker?

Arrow confirmed. He sniffed it and, *crunch*, it was gone.

"I knew it!" pointing to the empty spot Arrow was now licking.

"What are you talking about?" Ellison sounded tired. He was probably ready to go home and *read* about adventures instead of having them.

"Midge was here. I had a weird feeling she was following us."

"Why would she follow us? And why haven't we seen her on the way back?"

I remembered how suspicious she was acting at the stop sign. And I *had* spied a cheesy cracker on the shelter step after our emergency meeting.

Arrow had eaten that evidence too.

I smacked my forehead. "She must have sneaked down into the shelter shaft and overheard us planning the coyote hunt. Our voices would have echoed up the stairwell."

"Oh, man, and we know how she loves coyotes," Ellison said. "Maybe she was going to try to stop us."

My stomach did a nervous flip. "She probably didn't see us run into the woods after Arrow and Fang. Maybe she kept following the main trail thinking she'd catch up to us." I held out the end of the leash to Ellison. "I've gotta go back and find her. Will you take Arrow home?" I trusted Ellison almost as much as I trusted my mom and dad.

He nodded and took the end of the clothesline leash . . . again. "I'll give him a good brush and a long drink."

"When you get to my house, tell my mom we'll be home before dark. Midge can't be far."

Ellison pulled his peg shooter out of his pocket and handed it to me. "Here, just in case. I'm a lousy shot anyway."

I shoved the peg shooter into my back pocket.

It was time to say goodbye to Arrow. I tried not to think of saying goodbye Saturday for the last time. I knelt down and carefully ran my hand down his back, swiping away the dried leaves and dust.

He panted, so I poured water into my palm again while he lapped it up.

"See you soon, boy." Looking into his watery eyes to let him know I meant business, I said, "Go with Ellison."

Arrow's wet nose bumped my forehead. He seemed happy to obey.

"Midge!" I called her name as I ran back up the main trail, sure I'd catch up to her in a few minutes. Once again, I came to the side trail. Something made me stop and glance down the narrow dirt path.

What if Midge took this route when she didn't see us up head of her?

I stepped cautiously onto the side trail.

Nothing in sight but green and more green. The path was barely wide enough for a skinny fifth grader. The weeds and grasses were as tall as my head and way over my sister's.

About ten ladybug bootsteps ahead of me, a gray squirrel stood on its haunches, nibbling something between its paws. He stopped crunching and stared at me. He was clutching something too orange to be a nut.

Another cheesy goldfish cracker!

"Midge!" I hollered. My voice seemed to get caught in the thick green leaves.

The squirrel bolted.

I ran to the spot where he'd been munching my sister's favorite snack. Orange crumbs lay in the dust. Had she really gone this way all by herself?

I pushed ahead, sure the forest was closing in behind me the deeper I went.

The sunlight slashed across the bottoms of the lowest leaves of the trees and the tops of the weeds and wildflowers. The sun would be setting in an hour or so. I wouldn't find Midge in the dark. And I might not find my way back.

I thought of all the things that could be dangerous—the deep ponds and sloughs (basically a swamp), the mucky wetlands, and . . . the coyotes. They were awake when kids were supposed to be tucked in bed.

My insides became a swarm of moths knocking themselves into a porch light. The knapsack slumped down my wet back. I scoured the path for sight of the next orange fish-shaped cracker, telling myself . . .

Midge will be squatted next to a flower watching a bee collect pollen.

Midge will give up the search and be coming around the next bend.

Midge . . . was nowhere in sight.

26

S.T.O.P.P.

Noe's voice echoed in my head. *S.T.O.P.P.*

Right. Survival skill number one in any emergency situation.

Stop.

I stood still as a fly on a frog's nose.

Think.

So far, despite my insides bumping around like nervous moths, I'd made a logical choice to follow this path. I named off all the things I had in my knapsack: half a bottle of water, granola bar, rain poncho, glow stick.

Observe.

The woods were quieter here. I couldn't hear the distant *whoosh* of cars. That meant I was farther back into the woods than the main trails probably went. I didn't see any more crackers or other signs Midge had stayed on this path.

My stomach gave a deep growl. This was no time to crave cheesy snacks.

Plan.

Stay on this path for at least fifteen more minutes. Leave trail signs! Midge had been smart enough to leave a trail of fish crackers. Or maybe she was just sharing with the squirrels.

Pray.

"God." I said it out loud and it made me feel better. "I don't know where Midge is. Or where I am, even. But You do. Can You help us end up in the same uncharted territory at the same time? Oh, and please keep Midge safe till I get there."

No one was happier to be my hiking buddy than the mosquito buzzing in my ear. He must have used it as a megaphone because pretty soon more were buzzing around my head.

The trail led me through the tall oaks and pines but disappeared in a grove of squatty, tangled trees. With some trimming, the trees would have made a great fort. In the dying light, they'd make a good hiding place for unseen things that woke you up in the middle of the night.

I wound through the small, twisted branches and out again. The dirt path didn't reappear. But the ground seemed trampled flat. Maybe by deer moving from place to place or hikers going off trail. I followed it for a few minutes. It ended at the top of a small slope. Flat rocks and tree roots worked as a kind of staircase down to a wide and shallow creek. It would have been a fun place to watch minnows swim around your bare feet. And the perfect place to catch frogs.

I hoped that meant one thing.

I scrambled down the rocky slope to the edge of the water. The sun shone through the trees and reflected like scattered gold coins across the mossy rocks. Minnows darted away from me. Small green frogs squeaked and leaped into deeper water.

I scanned the creek to the left. This end curved around the shrubby bank across from me. The end to my right disappeared into thick trees on either side of the creek. Things sure disappeared a lot in the woods.

I looked back and forth again and again the way you do when you're crossing the street for the first time by yourself.

No Midge.

The moths started again in my belly. Then they fluttered up into my chest and into my brain, scrambling everything that had made sense fifteen minutes ago. Or had it been longer? At least standing in the open creek made the world seem less dark.

I took a deep breath in, then yelled, "MIIIDGE!"

Not a peep. Only the trickle of the creek and a woodpecker sending what sounded like Morse code.

The sun was going down on my left. That meant I was facing north and the creek, at least here, was running east to west. I figured this must be the same creek that ran through the bottom of the ravine Arrow made a narrow escape out of. I wondered if it ran all the way to the park where we hunted frogs.

Would Midge wonder that too? Would she think to follow the creek in case it brought her to the park near our house? She was smart, but still only eight. Her Native Illinois Flower Identification badge probably wouldn't come in too handy right now.

I decided to walk east along the creek. I'd only gone about five steps when I saw it. An arrow on the ground. Three branches about as long as my arm pointed in the exact direction I was heading. At the tip of the arrow was a rock, and under it, an empty fish cracker bag.

I started to run.

The creek curved. It turned narrow and muddy, then wider and deeper.

Mostly, I was able to stay close to it. After what seemed like forever, the creek flattened again, and I spotted another arrow on the bank. This one was made of rocks.

I broke into a trot. My legs and arms felt like rubber. Hanging over a ravine will do that to a guy. Plus, I hadn't eaten for hours. I'd stop in a minute and dig out my last camp granola bar. But first, I called out to Midge again.

Hmm. Was that a dove cooing? Or a tiny voice in the distance?

The sound gave me a burst of energy. I lurched into a stumble. Circling my arms wildly, I tried to get my feet back under me. Instead, my left foot slipped on a mossy rock, my ankle twisted, and I fell half in, half out of the shallow water.

A lightning bolt of pain shot up my leg.

I didn't even get a chance to try not to cry. The pain squeezed the tears right out of me. Everything turned blurry. Which was okay because I didn't want to look at my foot in case it was facing the wrong direction or something.

But I couldn't lose this chance to get Midge's attention if she was nearby.

I pressed my fingers between my lips and whistled, kind of. My mouth was dry; my hands were shaking. I took a slow deep breath in and tried again. I blew the loudest, longest whistle I could.

Quiet. A chatter of a squirrel overhead. The trickle of water under my soaked pant leg. A faint voice from up the creek.

I held my breath for a second. "Midge?" Then louder. "Midge?!"

"Jack?!"

"I'm back this way!" I gritted my teeth and scooted myself onto the pebbly bank.

Small splashes made their way toward me. Midge appeared on the bank—face red and sweaty, skinny arms scratched and dotted with mosquito bites, and ladybug boots covered in mud.

I held out my arms.

She slipped and splashed her way toward me, fell onto her knees, and threw her arms around my neck.

I'd found her!

"I found you!" she cried.

I didn't argue. I was too relieved to see her. Plus, we needed to make a plan, and fast.

She pulled back and said, "Hey, why are you playing in the creek? We need to get home before dark, or we'll be in big trouble."

I told her the bad news. "I really messed up my ankle, and the sun is going to set soon."

She carefully lifted the hem of my jeans and peeked at my ankle. "Eww, grooosss!"

"What? What? Is there blood? Is my foot backward?"

"No, your ankle looks like an eggplant," she said, screwing up her face. "I *hate* eggplant."

I peered through one squinted eye. The rubber tip of my gym shoe was pointed up and was scuffed and muddy as usual. Phew.

"But your head is on backward," she added.

"Gee, thanks for the encouragement."

Midge shrugged. "I'm a biologist, not a pediatrician."

27

FIRST RULE
OF SURVIVAL

Lightning bugs flashed green warnings around us. It was getting dark.

Maybe Mom was already out looking for us. Her long brown hair would be pulled back in her "let's get to work" ponytail. Maybe Ellison's dad would be with her, still dressed in his usual snazzy work suit. Maybe Mr. Bruno with his giant flashlight. Maybe even the police!

Then again, I'd told Ellison to tell my mom that Midge and I would be home before dark. Mom would be starting to worry.

If it was still light out and I didn't have an eggplant for

an ankle, I could have retraced my steps. What if we were stuck here for the night? We'd need shelter.

Midge found a sturdy piece of branch I could use as a crutch. Between leaning on that and holding on to Midge's bony shoulders, I was able to make my way up the embankment and into a thick patch of trees.

"First rule of survival," I said. "We need to build a shelter."

Midge helped me sit down at the base of a huge tree. She pulled a bag of fish crackers out of her knapsack and handed it to me. "Second rule of survival."

I had to admit, munching on junk food and actually having my little sister do everything I told her was kind of fun. She even seemed to be having fun making a shelter.

The tree I sat under had a low branch hanging right over my head. Perfect for the top of our shelter.

Midge spread my rain poncho underneath it. Then she gathered every loose branch she could find and leaned them against the limb on both sides.

I sat on the ground, trying to arrange them from the inside as Midge built the shelter around me. Finally, she hung her poncho over the open end of the shelter. It might not keep anything out, but I know it made both of us feel better.

She plopped onto our poncho rug and slid off her ladybug boots, tipping each one over to the side until the trickle of water stopped.

Too wiped out to talk, we sat facing each other, crunching crackers and taking small sips from our water bottles. (I'd given most of mine to Arrow.)

A ghost of moonlight filled the shelter. We were shadows in the dark.

For a second, I wished I had a walkie-talkie like Roger to call in a 10-20 to my mom. That is, if I had actually known where we were.

Midge sniffed. "What if no one finds us?"

"Of course someone will find us. I found you"—Midge cleared her throat loudly—"Fine, you found me, didn't you?"

"What if it's dangerous out here?" Her voice was shaky.

This was a giant forest preserve in the suburbs, not the Alaskan wilderness. Sure, there were coyotes. And maybe a bully who claimed the forest was *his* territory.

I bent my right leg and slowly worked the wet shoelace out of my even wetter gym shoe.

"Hand me your glow stick," I said. I heard Midge rustle around in her knapsack.

Snap. Crack. The green light appeared in her hands as she bent the plastic stick in several places to activate the fluorescent gel inside. She handed it to me.

I held it longways against my water bottle and tied it in place with the shoelace.

"Instant nightlight," I said, setting it between us. "Try to get some sleep."

I lay on my back, trying hard not to move my ankle.

Midge curled up on her side with her nose nearly pressed against the nightlight. Her face glowed green. "It's a *Lamprigera*," she whispered.

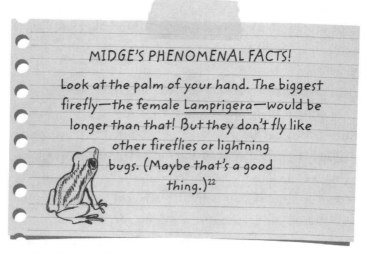

MIDGE'S PHENOMENAL FACTS!

Look at the palm of your hand. The biggest firefly—the female <u>Lamprigera</u>—would be longer than that! But they don't fly like other fireflies or lightning bugs. (Maybe that's a good thing.)[22]

"Ohhh—kay." I needed a distraction from my throbbing ankle, so I said, "I get the 'lamp' part but . . ."

She blinked her eyelids at me like she was sending *Duh, this is an easy one* in Morse code.

"A lightning bug!" I yelped.

Midge smiled, then yawned. "A firefly as big your hand."

I stared up at our ceiling of sticks. Slivers of full moon sneaked through our tree-branch ceiling.

"I'm cold," Midge murmured. She was still curled up on her side, staring at our homemade nightlight.

I pulled my empty knapsack out from under my head—it made a lousy pillow anyway—and spread it over her shoulder.

"I wish coyote would bring fire."

I wondered if I should tell her a different story. "Hey," I whispered. "Remember when you were two and ate a lightning bug?"

"He was so cute!"

"You thought it would make your tummy light up. Grandma put it in your hand and told you to be careful. Ten seconds later your lips were glowing. When she asked you what happened, you said, 'I kissed him and kissed him and kissed him.'"

Our laughing made the whole woods go quiet.

Maybe things are funnier when you're worn out. And it's dark, and you're somewhere you don't belong. And you're sleeping in a stick hut instead of a bed, with roots digging into your back. And you're not sure what to do next, except believe God is taking care of you.

28

THE HOT DOG TRAP

Something woke me up.

My eyes peeled open. I couldn't see much, but I heard Midge's soft snores. She was breathing through her mouth.

I once read that you unknowingly swallow six hundred and forty spiders over your lifetime.[23] The odds of that happening in the woods were even better. I reached over and carefully pushed her mouth closed, just in case. I figured eating one lightning bug had been enough, plus we had one granola bar left and who knew how many fish crackers.

No need to get desperate. Yet.

It was still dark, but the dark gray kind, right before morning. What had woken me up?

Yodels, yelps, yowls—coyote talk.

Midge popped up, more awake than I was. "I gotta go." Before I could stop her, she stepped right into her ladybug boots and scrambled out of the poncho door.

"Wait!" I hollered. "It might not be safe!" I rolled onto my right side and grabbed my walking stick. My ankle wasn't hurting as much as last night, so I was able crawl out of the shelter without pain shooting all the way up to my front teeth.

Would I find our shelter surrounded by a pack of predators? I didn't know, but I had to protect my sister. And I had to "go" too.

From what I could make out in the dim light, the coast looked clear. Wispy patches of mist floated around the black tree trunks. The odd shapes of things in the shadows reminded me of that morning in the cemetery.

Using the stick and the tree limb of our shelter, I pulled myself upright. I didn't venture far.

"Talk to me so I know where you are," I called. "And watch out for poison ivy." And Fang, I wanted to say but didn't.

A faint howl came from behind a tree about ten feet away. "Midge!"

Midge's voice came from the same direction. "I was letting you know where I was."

I heaved a sigh of relief.

My growling stomach told me the sun was about to come up. So did the pink, which was smeared like sidewalk chalk dust across the sky. Even though it was the end of summer, I shivered in the damp air.

I must've really been wishing for a campfire because I smelled wood smoke. And roasted hotdogs. Those smells couldn't be my stomach's imagination. They seemed to waft their way to me from the creek.

I hobbled over the forest floor. The layers of leaves and twigs and weeds now felt like an obstacle course. I made my way to the edge of the small hill that sloped down to the water.

On the bank across the creek, a small fire burned inside a circle of stones. I hadn't imagined it.

Two long sticks with a hot dog stuck on each end were propped over the low flames. The dripping juice hissed when it hit the fire. My mouth filled with water.

"I told you." Midge ran up beside me. "Coyote brought us a fire!"

Well, someone had brought us Oscar Mayer, anyway. I wasn't interested in giving coyotes credit for anything.

But who was cooking breakfast?

"I guess they won't earn their Super Steward badge," Midge said.

She was right. It was against the rules to build a fire in the forest preserve. Who would break an important rule like that?

"I bet this is Buzz's territory," Midge whispered. "He

probably lives right across the creek in a cave and eats bugs and frogs."

What if it was a trap? I could see it now . . .

. . . Starving and limping, we creep up to the fire. We each reach out, hands shaking from fear and hunger. We clutch the ends of the sticks and—thwap!—set off a chain reaction . . .

1. *Wire connected to end of hot dog stick, tripped by . . .*
2. *Movement of hot dog toward watering mouth, releases . . .*
3. *Giant cage made out of branches, falls . . .*
4. *Out of tree branches overhead and, bam . . .*
5. *Jack and his annoying little sister, captured!*

. . . Then Buzz springs out of the thick bushes, snarling and slobbering. He shoves his face between the stick bars of our cage. His yellow eyes glare at me as he snaps, "Toast!"

After all, Buzz seemed like the kind of kid less interested in earning a Super Steward badge and more interested in a badge for, say, cannibalism.

"What if it's a trap?" This time I said it out loud.

Midge shook her head the way Mom does when it's obvious—except to me—that I'm wrong. "Nobody who steals frogs from little girls could be that creative."

My growling stomach agreed. "Fine. Let's pack up quick and prevent a forest fire."

Five minutes later, we were living out my imagined

scenario. We hobbled down the embankment, and Midge waded across the creek to the opposite bank. She took off her boots and filled them with water. Barefoot, she scurried over to the fire, held the boots above it, and dumped the water over the small campfire. The flames sputtered. The hot dogs dripped creek water.

But my gnawing stomach still growled at them.

No matter *who* was breaking fire safety rules, we'd figured a trade was only fair. Midge set our last granola bar and Ellison's peg shooter on a rock beside the dying fire. Then she stepped back into her wet boots and snatched the hot dog skewers.

Phew! No cages fell out of the tree branches hanging over her head.

She splashed back across the water.

"Good work," I said, "you just earned the Fire Putter-outer badge." I pretended to pin it on her wrinkled, mud-splattered shirt. "Sorry it's invisible."

She handed me one of the sticks. We nibbled and ouched our way through the still-hot hot dogs in seconds. We needed to get out of here before Buzz—or whoever the rule-breaker was—appeared out of the woods.

Going back the way we'd come yesterday would have been the safest plan. But . . .

. . . Fang was still out there. And maybe Capt. Beans.

How great would it be to find her and emerge from the woods with her furry ginger head sticking out of the top of my knapsack? The Hunt for Fang would at least end in an awesome rescue. Besides finding my sister, of course.

Continuing the hunt—even if it was now just my one-man secret mission—meant heading into uncharted territory.

29

"I'M A GIANT BREAKFAST SAUSAGE"

The sun rose to our right, flooding the creek bed with light.

With the end of my walking stick, I drew a map in the mud. "I'm betting this creek is connected to the creek in the park. The sun is rising over that end of the creek, which means that's east. If we head in that direction, we should eventually reach the park."

We walked and limped toward the rising sun, as fast as our three legs would carry us.

After we were clear of what may have been Buzz's campsite, we stopped to rest. The morning was already warm and humid.

While I took a small sip of my stale water, Midge gathered rocks. She squatted next to me and laid the rocks in a straight line. Two shorter lines of rocks at the top would point anyone who found the arrow in our direction. Including Buzz.

"In case someone comes looking for us," she said.

Hopefully not the guy who missed breakfast, I thought.

My ankle was throbbing, but I concentrated on keeping the sun ahead of us as the creek zigzagged through the forest. Sometimes we had to cross the shallow parts or walk up into the woods if the water was over our shins.

After what seemed like forever, but was probably only as long as it takes me to down a third helping of pancakes, we stopped to sip the last of our water.

"Jack?"

"Hmm?" I draped my arm back over Midge's shoulders for support.

She wrapped her scrawny arm around my waist. "I'm mad at you for trying to hunt the coyote."

Now wasn't a good time to mention that I hadn't given up yet.

"But if I were Pastor Noe, I'd award you the Super Steward badge anyway," she said, keeping me steady every time I teetered on the uneven ground. "You're taking good care of me."

"Thanks, Midge," I said, not taking my eyes off the path we were forging. "You're taking good care of me too."

"Believe it or not," she said, her boots squelching along beside me, "it's way easier than catching frogs."

Nothing looked familiar. I mean except for every tree looking like every other tree. I didn't know if this was the creek that led to the park. Or if it would take us get us back to our family. Maybe Fang felt the same walking down Cherry Avenue.

Midge let loose a long howl that nearly busted my eardrums.

"What was that for?"

"I'm being one with nature," she said. "You should try it. You're kind of uptight."

I made a mental list of good reasons why: a failed hunt, a messed up ankle, a night in the woods, and the worst . . . Arrow's real owner. He'd be here tomorrow. And Arrow wouldn't be mine anymore.

"Is it because you're gonna miss the Super Steward scavenger hunt today?" Midge asked.

ARGH! The scavenger hunt! How could I have forgotten? The bus with all the kids would probably be arriving at the main trailhead of the forest preserve in the next couple hours. Even if we could make it out of the woods in time, I wouldn't be hiking with a twisted ankle.

Aw, what the heck? I tilted my head back and howled the loudest, loneliest, and saddest howl the woods had ever heard.

"Good one!" Midge sounded genuinely impressed.

I even felt a little better. After all, now things definitely couldn't get any worse.

"Whoa," Midge said like she was riding a horse. She stopped in her—our—tracks.

I leaned hard onto the hiking stick to keep my balance. "Hey, I don't need another twisted ankle. Why did you stop?" Then I saw what she was "whoa-ing" about.

About twenty limps ahead, a huge tree tilted over the edge of the creek. Half of its roots crawled out of the ground toward the water. The other half hung on for dear life to the side of the embankment that rose up to our right.

Peeking out from under the slanted tree trunk was a small coyote. Maybe a few inches taller than Arrow.

My crossbow was lost. Ellison's peg shooter had been traded for a hot dog. All I had was my hiking stick.

The coyote crept out into the open, not taking its yellow eyes off of us. It cocked its head to the side just like Arrow does when he's curious. The ridiculously big ears pricked and twitched.

I wondered if they could hear my heart thumping.

It took a couple careful steps toward us.

"Wow, Jack," Midge whispered, "you must have said, 'I'm a giant breakfast sausage' in coyote."

A loud rustle of grass and snap of twigs came from the woods. Another—bigger—coyote flew out of the brush growing along the bank. He pounced onto the smaller one, and they tumbled together into the shallow water.

"Typical big brother," Midge said.

The big one jumped up. He shook the water from his brown-and-gray fur. He was twice the size of his sibling, but still looked pretty young and scrawny. I guess he hadn't hit puberty either.

The smaller coyote slipped its way over the slimy rocks, yipping and nipping at her brother's back leg.

"Typical little sister," I said.

Just then, the bigger one looked straight at us.

It was Fang.

I remembered that morning in the cemetery, how Midge had jumped up and down and hollered to spook him. I couldn't jump. So, holding on to my stick, I let go of

Midge's shoulder and waved my arm back and forth over my head. "We're not breakfast!" I hollered.

Midge joined in . . . kind of. "Watch out! *Homo sapiens* on the loose!" she shouted, making a shooing motion. "Jack's armed! And I don't mean the skinny one flapping in the air."

The pup tripped over itself trying to escape across the creek toward the opposite bank. Fang bolted too, splashing through the water . . . and right past his sister. We watched the pup stumble over the slippery, mossy rocks, yelping and trying to catch up.

That's when we saw her. The biggest coyote yet. And the toughest of all species: Mom. She rushed to the pup.

Fang hung at the edge of the woods across the creek. I wondered if he felt like I did—like maybe he should've done a better job taking care of his sister.

The mother glared our way and barked a warning. This was her territory.

Just like Cherry Avenue was mine, well . . . and Midge's, Mom and Dad's, and Mr. Bruno's. Maybe even Fang's. I remembered what Noe had said, everything is God's. My neighborhood, the woods, my family, and Fang and his family.

A wild barking sounded behind us. More coyotes? We were surrounded!

I cranked around, sending a shooting pain up my leg.

Arrow was making a beeline toward me. Rushing up the bank farther behind him were Ellison, Mr. Henry, and Hank, the forest ranger from camp.

Arrow must have spied the coyotes. He shot forward, barking like crazy.

Only I stood between him and the mother, little pup, and Fang.

"Arrow," I barely croaked his name, "come!" I dropped my hiking stick and opened my arms, praying he'd obey.

He swerved and leaped . . . right into my arms.

I lost my balance, but Midge grabbed my shirt to keep me from falling. "Look, they're running home," she said, pointing behind me

Arrow was nearly licking my face off, but I teetered back around to face the coyotes.

Three fluffy tails disappeared into the woods. Mother, pup . . . and Fang . . . were gone. And so far, still, was Capt. Beans.

30

FETCH!

Hank radioed in that we'd been found safe and (mostly) sound. Then he checked us over to make sure we weren't seriously hurt. He squatted down to take a closer look at my ankle. "Your ankle looks like an eggplant," he said, as everyone else gathered close to see.

Midge squatted down beside Hank. "That was my professional opinion as well," she said.

Sheesh, what was the deal with nature-types and gross vegetables?

Just as I was getting uncomfortable about my eggplant being on display, Hank told us we needed to get back to the main trail. And he would have to carry me if we were going to cover any ground.

Talk about embarrassing. Nothing like a piggyback ride to hurt a guy's pride.

Thank goodness Ellison didn't seem to notice. As we trudged uphill, weaved through the weeds and trees, and navigated roots and rocks and fallen branches, he kept asking me questions: How did I track down Fang? Did I defend myself with the peg shooter? Was sleeping in the woods scary? Did we have to eat grubs to survive?

In the same kind of book-quotey voice Ellison always used, Mr. Henry said: "'He learned the most important rule of survival, which was that feeling sorry for yourself didn't work.'"[24]

"*Hatchet!*" Ellison blurted, like he was answering a trivia question.

"Author?" his dad quizzed.

"Easy. Gary Paulsen."

They high-fived.

"Jack didn't even need a hatchet to build our shelter," Midge said. "He had me."

"That deserves a special badge," Ellison said.

Like maybe the We-Wouldn't-Have-Needed-a-Shelter-if-Midge-Hadn't-Got-Lost badge, I wanted to say. But, then, I had to admit Midge wouldn't have followed us in the first place if I hadn't planned the hunt.

In fact, she told us how she did it. After Midge had seen

us ditch our bikes, she hid her bike and helmet behind some trees. She was following us on foot when the Brownie troop came along on their nature hike.

"They were the perfect camouflage," said Midge. "Short, noisy, and cute. But I lost you when you ran after Arrow. Then I saw the little dirt trail . . ."

I imagined her venturing down the path, believing I had gone the same way. Ouch. I felt like I'd just been awarded the Rotten Brother badge.

After a slow trek over the mushy and leafy ground, we reached the main trail. Hank set me down, and Mr. Henry put an arm around me to prop me up.

Hank trotted up the trail. His dark-green forest pre-serve truck was parked to the side. He backed it up, parked beside us, and hopped out. He pulled a first-aid kit from under the seat and then checked my ankle again.

I gritted my teeth.

Definitely a bad sprain, he said—but probably not bro-ken. He set a cold pack on the puffiest part, then he care-fully wound a long, stretchy bandage around it.

He helped me into the front seat, and Ellison put Arrow on my lap. We sat in between Hank and Mr. Henry. Midge and Ellison crawled in behind us.

The truck lumbered along the wide, gravel trail. Arrow bounced between curling up on my lap and stepping across

Mr. Henry to stick his head out the window.

"Jack?! Midge?!" Mom's voice crackled over the dash-board radio. "Are you okay? I've been praying all night."

Hank unhooked the microphone attached to the stretchy radio cord and handed it to me.

I pressed the button on the side and talked into the mic. "Copy that, Mom. We're fine. We, uh, learned a lot." (Moms always love when you learn stuff.) "And we didn't get rabies. Over."

"Jack's ankle looks like an eggplant!" Midge hollered over my shoulder. "Oh! And we saw a whole family of—"

I let go of the talk button before Mom could hear Midge say "coyotes."

"Thank the Lord you're safe! No rabies, one sprained ankle, zero more adventures today." (Moms are also all about lists.) "I've been going crazy at home in case you came back there. I just got the call that you'd been found. I'm waiting at the main trailhead now."

Poor Mom. And here she was worried about rabies.

"Big 10-4," I said. Roger would have been impressed with my walkie-talkie lingo. I handed the mic back to Hank.

"Mr. Hank, guess what?" Midge piped up from the back. "Coyote brought us fire, just like in your story."

Hank glanced down at me. His eyebrow arched so high above his eye it almost looked like a question mark.

"Either that," Midge babbled on, "or we ate Buzz Rublatz's breakfast."

"I'll fill you in later," I whispered to Hank. Then, "How did you find us, anyway?"

Ellison was apparently dying to tell the story. "When you weren't home by dark, your mom called my mom." Ellison rattled on like he was telling me about a new book he was reading. "So I explained that you were looking for Midge. Then Dad called the forest preserve police. Hank put together a small search team, but it was way after dark by then. People took turns looking through the night, and Dad and Arrow and I joined the search early this morning."

"Your mother will be relieved to see you," added Mr. Henry. "Your father arrived home during the night but has been searching with another ranger on a different part of the main trail."

"Thanks to Ellison," Hank said, "I had a rough idea of where you may have gone into the woods. But when you left the trail, I had no way of knowing which way you went. Once the sun was up, I found your shelter. I walked down to the creek and was radioing the station to report in. That's when I heard Mr. Henry and his son calling your name from the woods behind me."

Ellison leaned forward and shook my shoulder. "You want to know the best part of the story? I told Arrow,

'Fetch Jack!' And he did. He finally fetched!"

Hearing his name, Arrow dropped down from the window and curled up on my lap.

"Good job, boy. You found me. Again."

His tail gave a tired wag.

31

NO CAPT. BEANS

When we pulled into the parking lot at the main trail-head, Mom and Dad were the first people I spotted. They stood at the back of Dad's pickup truck with an arm around each other. They were talking with a man dressed like Hank. Another forest preserve truck, an ambulance—and a police car—were parked nearby.

"Uh-oh," Midge said. "Mr. Hank, if I'm gonna be locked up, can it be in the zoo?"

A laugh burst out of Mr. Henry that made Arrow jump up and wag his tail. "No one is going to jail," he said, "or to the zoo."

"Aw, fish sticks," she whined.

"Those are just some of the folks who were out looking for you," Hank said.

Dad was taking a cup of coffee from the ranger. His clothes were dirty and wet in the sweaty spots. Mom's long brown hair was loose and messy, like she'd combed her fingers through it a hundred times. She was wearing the same clothes from yesterday, same as Midge and I were. If it had been a normal day, she would have told me, "Change your shirt. You're a Finch, not a hamper."

Besides the search team, the church bus was already parked on the other side of the lot.

Noe and the staff were circled together with their heads bowed. They would know by now we'd been lost. All the campers stood in little groups beside the bus. Some kids looked like they might be praying. Some were fidgeting and giggling.

Mom spotted us and waved her arms over her head even though Hank was already backing the truck into a parking spot nearby. She and Dad ran to meet us, hugging and kissing Midge and me the second we emerged from the truck.

Dad carried me over to his truck and set me on the open tailgate. Arrow leaped right up beside me. Midge climbed up on the other side of me.

The paramedics checked us over and agreed my eggplant

was probably a sprained ankle. They told Mom I should get an X-ray, but that we didn't need to go to the hospital.

After we got the all clear, Ellison waved his arms in the direction of the scavenger hunters. Roger and Ruthie broke away from the group and ran toward us.

Following a second attack of hugs and questions and pats on the back, all us kids sat on the bed of the truck, sucking on the juice boxes Mom handed out.

My story spilled out, as noisy and colorful as a box of LEGO blocks onto the metal truck bed. When I got to the part about being face-to-face with the coyotes, Ruthie raised her eye patch. Maybe she needed both her eyes to hear what I'd say next.

She looked mostly straight at me.

I knew exactly what she was wondering. "Sorry," I said, shaking my head. "No sign of Capt. Beans."

She flipped her eye patch back down. I realized it had a small piece of paper stuck to it. In red marker were the words: Save Jack and Midge.

"Thanks for trying to find her, Jack," Ruthie said. "I'm glad you and Midge are okay. Family is the most important thing."

Noe jogged over and high-fived Midge and me at the same time. "Hey, little dudes, we've been praying for you two since we got here. Your mama told us what happened."

He turned toward all the scavenger hunters across the parking lot, lifted two thumbs up, and bellowed. "They're okay!"

Everyone cheered.

The camp staffers started singing "He's Got the Whole World in His Hands."

And, then, a howl rose up from the pack of Cunning Coyotes.

Midge stood up behind me on the bed of the truck. She answered them with a long, yodeling howl.

Ellison, Roger, Ruthie, and I—and even Arrow—joined in.

I please-please-pleased my parents into letting me stay until the scavenger hunt was over. At least I'd get to see which team won the Super Steward badge.

Even though Midge was a Cunning Coyote, Noe agreed to let her take my place on our Radical Ranger team. Besides, my record of success lately wasn't so great. My team had a better shot at winning without me.

"We're going to win the Super Steward badge for you,"

Ellison said, slapping me on the back and hopping off the tailgate. "Right, guys?"

Roger, Ruthie, and even Midge agreed.

"You kids are already Super Stewards," said Mr. Henry. He gave Ellison a side hug, then said he was heading home to let Mrs. Henry know we were okay.

Across the parking lot, Noe directed the staff through his megaphone. The bigger kids organized all the scavenger hunters into their teams and lined them up at the start of the main trailhead.

The Tree Street Kids headed over to join the hunt without me.

A few minutes later, I spied Buzz. His spiky hair stuck up above the crowd, and his team stepped up in line behind Ellison, Midge, Roger, and Ruthie. Even though I couldn't tell if he was looking at me, I had a feeling his breath didn't smell like hot dogs this morning. In fact, I could swear he was munching on a granola bar, just like the one we had left next to the soggy campfire.

I wasn't sorry we'd put the fire out, whether it was Buzz's or not.

Noe lifted his megaphone and read from the Bible about how God created men and women in His own image. He made them stewards of the earth and told them to take care of it.

"'Rule over the fish in the sea and the birds in the sky and over *every* living creature that moves on the ground.' . . . 'I give you every seed-bearing plant on the face of the whole earth and every tree that has fruit with seed in it.' . . . God saw all that he had made, and it was very good."[25]

All that God made was very good. I knew that had to include mosquitoes, and even coyotes.

Then a whistle sounded, and the scavenger hunt began.

32

THE SURVIVAL BADGE

Hank shook my hand before he left and walked back to his truck.

"Thanks for finding us," I said.

He nodded. "We all helped each other. Just like Cougar, Fox, Squirrel, Antelope, Frog"—he pointed at me—"and Coyote."

Arrow perked his ears up.

I figured Midge was Frog. But me, a coyote?

I must've looked doubtful because Hank said, "Smart, resourceful, protective of family . . . Yup. Coyote."

Dad finished up talking to the police officer and walked over to shake Hank's hand. "Thank you, again."

Hank nodded and headed toward his truck.

Dad hopped onto the tailgate and sat on the other side of Arrow. He was more quiet than usual. He reached over Arrow and draped his arm across my shoulders. He smelled even more manly than I did. "Those woods are scary at night," he said. His voice was low and tired. "We'll talk more about your forest adventures later. I'm just thankful we're all together again and safe."

Before I could answer, Mom appeared with a crumpled brown grocery bag. She emptied one thing at a time onto the end of tailgate—a half jar of peanut butter, leftover hamburger buns, a few red apples, and—ugh—cheesy fish crackers. "I didn't have time to make sandwiches before the police officer drove me over here, so I just tossed supplies into the bag and . . . where did I put that plastic knife . . . ?"

She talked like she does when she's trying not to cry. Fast and with lots of details.

"You'd make a good survivalist, Mom," I said, twisting the lid off the peanut butter jar.

She pulled the plastic knife out of her back pocket and smiled. "Every mom is a survivalist, sweetie."

After the hunt, all the kids gathered in the trailhead picnic area. Dad, Mom, Arrow, and I snagged a front seat on one of the picnic benches.

"You've all worked hard and learned a lot this week," Noe said. "Being a Super Steward isn't just about knowing how to build a fire or even lots of Bible verses about God's creation. It's about care. And cooperation. Learning not to just take but to give back. To preserve the places God has set us in and to nurture what we find there."

The staff passed out a badge to everyone for participation. The winner of the scavenger hunt was one of the Radical Rangers teams, and the Super Steward badge was awarded to the team with the most points collected throughout the entire week of camp . . . one of the teams from the Cunning Coyotes.

Of course, they sent up an ear-splitting *YEEOOWWLL*!

I was disappointed we hadn't won, but it had been an adventure. And I didn't need a badge to prove that.

"And finally," Noe said, "we have a special badge to give out. This one goes to the team who put what they learned into practice. Navigation, collaboration, shelter building, and even rescue. Our honorary Mega Steward and Survival badge goes to—Jack, Ellison, Roger, Ruthie, and—littlest but not least—Midge!"

Mom drove me and Midge straight to the doctor. Midge argued that biologists were tougher than they looked, but was happy to snag extra suckers from the nurse. My ankle was badly sprained, so the doctor gave me a cool pair of metal crutches with rubber pads that dug into my armpits and smelled like tires.

When we got back home, Grandma and Grandpa were waiting for us. Grandma said she just had to hug us. Grandpa was impressed by my big fat ankle and our hunt for the coyote. Even though it a big fat failure.

Dad pointed out all the good things about our adventure: not having to resort to eating bugs, winning the Mega badge, and rescuing Arrow. (I didn't point out I shouldn't have taken him into the woods in the first place.)

And, best of all, Mom added, coming out of the woods safe and sound. Moms are all about "safe" and "sound."

I was wiped by the time I went to bed. I felt like I could sleep for days with Arrow's bony back curled against my chest. Plus, that way, we'd skip Saturday . . .

Doomsday. The day I would have to say goodbye to the dog that wasn't my dog.

Nope, Arrow wasn't my dog. He was my friend.

33

DOOMSDAY

Doomsday morning, Midge agreed to help me give Arrow a bath outside. While she did "most of the work," I sat on the grass beside the washtub with my crutches on the other side of me. My sprained ankle was wrapped up like a sausage, my bare toes burning in the sun.

We lifted Arrow out of the dirty bathwater and set him on the grass. He shook, spraying us all over. Then he made his escape and ran in circles around the yard, his fur drying in a flash in the hot sun.

He acted like he didn't have a care in the world. Like he was right where he belonged. Like we'd be friends forever.

And we would be friends forever. No matter where he was, I'd love him.

I clapped, and Arrow made his usual beeline for me. He knocked me over, stepping onto my chest and licking my nose.

Midge crawled over and petted and kissed him. I knew she'd miss him too. He wasn't a pet frog, but at least you could train a dog to "stay."

Too bad he couldn't stay.

The screen door squeaked. Dad trotted outside and down the back steps, clapping his hands too.

Arrow launched off my belly—*oof!*—and ran to him.

"Who's a good boy?" Dad said, stooping down to scratch Arrow behind the ears.

Arrow's back leg thumped spastically against the patio. Dad laughed. He walked over to us, and Arrow trotted behind him.

Dad helped me sit up and sat on the grass with us.

Arrow plopped onto my lap. He seemed floofed up and happy.

"You've done a good job of taking care of Arrow, son." Dad put his hand on my shoulder, his face serious. "And I'm proud of how you watched out for your sister in the woods."

I nodded. I felt squished between being crazy happy and rottenly sad.

A rumble shook the trees along Cherry Avenue. A semitruck strained and rumbled up the street and lurched to a halt and huff in front of the house, nearly taking some of the tree limbs with it.

Mom, Grandpa, and Grandma all hurried out of the house.

As Grandpa walked on across the front yard toward the huge truck, I held tight to Arrow. Like we were dangling from a cliff.

A few minutes later, Grandpa and the truck driver were walking toward us. Small and hunched, he looked more like a bendable action figure than a guy who drove a big rig.

When they reached the middle of the front yard, the man spied me sitting in the grass with the dog.

Arrow stiffened in my arms. He barked, knocking his head into my chin, and broke free. He ran at the truck driver, who teetered as he got down on one knee and held his arms open.

Arrow leaped and bounced around the man in between licking his hands and face. He twisted in midair, whining and whimpering and wagging his whole body. He was happier than I had ever seen him.

A lump sat in my throat.

"All right, all right, Sparky!" The man laughed until he had to swipe an arm across his slimed face.

"*Canis lupus familiaris 'sparkius,*'" said Midge, pulling up a handful of grass and throwing it at nothing. "Not as great a name as Tyrannocanis rex Arrow, but it's okay."

The man straightened, barely. He walked my way with Arrow nearly dancing around his feet.

Dad helped me stand up, and Grandpa introduced Mr. Davis.

"Young man, I'm grateful to you. This dog's my best friend"—he sniffed, grabbed a handkerchief from his back pocket, and blew his nose—"and you've taken good care of him, I see."

My voice cracked like an egg over that lump in my throat. "Yes, sir."

"'Except Jack never could get Arrow to fetch right," Midge said.

"Arrow, hmm?" Mr. Davis smiled. "Good name. It fits. 'Cuz don't I know that dog can take off like a shot."

Mr. Davis explained how he'd pulled over to check his load and Arrow had run off into the cornfield. He called and whistled for him for hours but finally had to give up and get back on the road.

"It was one of the hardest things I've ever had to do." Then his face brightened up. "One thing that ain't so hard is teaching a dog to fetch."

The trick to fetch, Mr. Davis said was "incentive." He reached into his shirt pocket and pulled out a cheddar cheese fish cracker.

34

CUTE-US KITTENUS

Mom invited Mr. Davis to stay for lunch. We all sat on the patio eating hot dogs. Ellison, Roger, and Ruthie showed up for moral support.

Ruthie smiled weakly at me. She knew exactly how it felt to lose a pet.

Arrow seemed to think she needed cheering up. He kept sniffing around her and nudging her hand.

While the grown-ups talked in low voices, we kids sat in the grass playing with Arrow. All I wanted to do was keep hugging him and telling him how much I'd miss him. I hoped he understood.

Everyone had a goodbye gift for Arrow. I mean, Sparky. Ellison had wrapped Hutch's old collar with a colorful book sox cover. Roger gave him a squeaky toy shaped like a newspaper, which Arrow was now gnawing and slobbering on.

And Ruthie handed me two small packages, one for me and even one for his owner—the picture she took of me and Arrow. Each copy was in a frame made out of Popsicle sticks and decorated with blue-and-green glitter.

I would have skipped the glitter, but it didn't matter.

"Looks like doggie Christmas over here," said Grandpa, as he walked over with Mr. Davis.

Everyone stood up. Ellison hoisted me upright.

Ruthie held out the other glittery framed picture to Mr. Davis. "Jack loves Arrow—I mean, Sparky. Can you set this in Sparky's dog bed so he never forgets Jack?" Then she mumbled, "Pictures help you to not forget."

Mr. Davis smiled, but seemed a little sad too. "I'll definitely put this beautiful picture and fancy frame in a very special place on my dashboard. But—"

Arrow barked at Ruthie and darted off in the direction of Mr. Bruno's house next door. He ran back to us.

Mr. Davis tried to finish what he was saying. "But I've been talking with your wonderful family, Jack, and watching Sparky enjoy this big yard . . . and all you kids—"

Arrow barked again at Ruthie.

She shrugged at me. "What did I do?"

Then he ran to the edge of Mr. Bruno's driveway and back again.

"Maybe he's teaching you to fetch," I joked.

Mr. Davis looked down at Arrow. "What is it, boy? You want to play fetch?"

At the sound of the word, Arrow barked at Ruthie and took off. This time he didn't stop at the edge of our backyard or Mr. Bruno's driveway. He just kept running.

"Arrow!" I hollered. When he didn't come right back, I hobbled after him as fast as I could, one good leg and two crutches making pretty good ground—across the driveway, around Mr. Bruno's garage, and into the long backyard.

"Sparky!" Mr. Davis called from behind me.

The shouts of everyone else followed me.

"Arrow!"

"What's happening?"

"Not again!"

But I didn't have to chase Arrow far. He stopped at the cover of the bomb shelter.

"What is it? What's down there?" I asked, hopping to get my balance.

He sniffed all around the cover. *"Rarf!"*

Everyone caught up and gathered around.

As soon as Ruthie was standing next to me, Arrow stopped sniffing and barked at her.

Ellison and Roger lifted up the shelter cover.

And Arrow, for the first time, ran right down the metal spiral staircase. All of us kids followed him. I went last, scooting down the steps on my backside.

Dad handed my crutches down to Ellison.

"What's all the fuss?" Mr. Bruno's voice joined everyone else's at the shelter opening above our heads.

At the bottom of the shaft, Arrow sniffed at the main door to the shelter room and barked again.

I put my hand on the door handle. Everyone crowed up against me.

Midge grabbed my arm. "Wait. What if Buzz is in there?" she whispered. "What if he invaded your territory because we ate his hot dogs?"

It was one thing to share our neighborhood and the woods with Fang. And even to share them with Buzz. But . . .

"Da Bomb Shelter is our secret fort. Impenetrable. No one could possibly invade—"

A weird growl sounded from inside the shelter. *"Mmm-rawrrr!"*

"Whoa! What was that?" Ellison hissed in my ear.

Arrow barked, then scratched at the door. He wagged his tail.

I took the wagging tail as a good sign. I took a deep breath and swung the door open.

All five of us tumbled through the doorway.

In the light coming down the shaft, we could see the shelter was empty.

No Buzz. Our shelter was still ours.

"*Mmm-rawrrr . . .*" The strange sound came from behind the snack cooler to our right. And funny squeaks, like balloons rubbing together.

Midge grabbed the camping lantern off the table. She switched on the light.

Arrow crept closer to the cooler, sniffing.

Ruthie followed him as we all watched.

Midge stepped closer to her and held the lantern high.

"Oh, my gosh!" Ruthie said and froze. After a few seconds, she turned to face us. In the lantern light, I could see she was crying. "It's Capt. Beans!"

"Okay, not so impenetrable," I said to Ellison and Roger.

"Now I guess it's girls *and* cats allowed," Roger whispered.

Midge peeked over the other side of the cooler. "*Felis catus* cute-us kittenus!" Midge announced. "Four of them!"

35

FURRY GIFTS

We all crowded around the cooler and peeked over.

Capt. Beans was curled protectively around four balls of fur: two gingers, a brown-and-black striped tabby, and a gray.

We refilled the water bowl we had in the shelter for Arrow, propped the main shelter door open, and quietly headed back up the stairs to report on our discovery.

The best we all could figure was that we'd left the shelter hatch open the other afternoon when we left on our hunt for Fang. Capt. Beans must have needed a safe place to have her kittens and made her way into the shelter after we were all gone.

Mr. Bruno said he'd noticed the hatch open, and when no one answered when he called down, he'd closed it, not realizing Capt. Beans was inside.

First, Mom scolded us about how dangerous that open hatch could have been for Mr. Bruno.

We all said a lot of "sorrys" for that.

Then Grandma and Ruthie went back down into the shelter to bring Capt. Beans some food and a clean towel to make a bed. Having been a farmer, Grandma knew all about animals.

Ellison, Roger, Midge, and I sat in the grass playing with Arrow. In all the excitement, I'd completely forgotten that it was past time for him to leave with Mr. Davis.

But when I looked over at the grown-ups, now sitting at Mr. Bruno's picnic table, he was nowhere to be seen.

Grandpa sauntered over. "Well, looks like you got that dog you prayed for."

We were all quiet while Arrow rolled over in the grass and four sets of hands scratched his belly. "What do you mean?" I could barely ask.

"Mr. Davis says living on the road is hard. For old, achy men . . . and for young pups. He saw how much you love Arrow, and he wants that dog to have the best life he can."

I still couldn't believe what my grandpa was telling me. How could anyone give up their dog?

"Arrow is your dog now," Grandpa said. "You do the

best job you can. Honor the gift you've been given."

I nodded. I scooped Arrow into my arms and hugged him.

"Kittens for everyone!" Ruthie announced. She spread photographs of the week-old kittens across Mr. Bruno's picnic table.

It was time for another Monday Tree Street Kids meeting and Ruthie's report.

Arrow sat next to me. He was now an official member.

We'd decided to meet around Mr. Bruno's picnic table until my ankle healed. Mom said I'd had enough adventures for the summer.

A guy really can't have too many adventures. But I supposed one sprained ankle was enough. The day after the kittens were born, Ruthie's dad decided the best thing to do with the baby Beanses would be to give them away to good homes. He'd offered free kittens to Mr. Bruno and to our family.

Any of the kittens except for one. Ruthie was keeping the tabby, the only girl kitten, so the mom and daughter could be together.

Mr. Bruno told us to decide which one he should keep.

Mr. Davis was happy to accept the offer after Dad called him. He said he'd be back in a few months to get the kitten. And to visit Arrow.

And Mom and Dad gave Midge permission to have her own pet.

Midge shuffled through the pictures on the table. "Well, it's not a cute, slimy frog," she said, "but this one looks cuddly too." She pointed to the photo of the scruffy gray kitten.

"What are you going to name it?" Ruthie asked.

I guessed Tyrannosaurus catus.

"He looks kind of wild," Roger said.

"He does," Ellison said. "Like a tiny coyote."

"That's it!" I was so excited about my idea I would have jumped out of my seat if I could have. "How about . . . ?"

Midge stared wide-eyed at me from across the picnic table and smiled. Together we shouted:

"Fang!"

"Does anyone second that motion?" Ellison asked, making the decision official.

Midge tilted her head back and howled in agreement.

The rest of us howled along, and Arrow joined right in.

THE END

ACKNOWLEDGMENTS

The narrow dirt path took my daughter and me deeper into the woods.

I'd hiked it only once before. I remembered how it had sloped down into a beautiful ravine carpeted with red and gold leaves.

Now they were winter gray.

Next, we trekked up a short, steep hill that ended at a cross path.

Go left or go right? I pointed left, knowing we'd eventually reach a shoulder-high wall of orange prairie grass. We followed the path through the leafless oaks and maples until we dead-ended at the prairie and again turned left. We'd eventually complete a lopsided rectangular course.

For now, the prairie grasses rustled on our right and the woods rose up on our left. Another deadish-end and we pivoted left and back into the forest.

"Mom," my daughter said, pointing at a furry pile of animal droppings. "Is that from a coyote?"

"Yeah, coyote scat," I said.

The animals often leave evidence of their presence near the borders of their territories. The actual coyotes are less easy to spy. But it was still a "fun" discovery (okay, not Disney World fun, but the kind of fun nature lovers have).

As we hiked on, my daughter a few steps ahead of me, I thanked God for the woods and how they inspired *The Hunt for Fang*.

My daughter halted. She pointed at the ground again.

!SPOILER ALERT!

In the dirt lay a cheesy fish-shaped cracker, the exact kind I describe Midge dropping along the path when she becomes lost in the woods.

We spied another cheesy fish cracker and then another— evidence of the presence of young hikers.

I was ridiculously excited. I felt I was standing at the border between my story world and my real world.

When is a cheesy fish-shaped cracker a gift from God? When it's also a sign to you that you're on the right path . . .

Thanks:

I'm thankful for the expansive forest preserve system in our region and for the people—many of whom are volunteers—who care for it so passionately. I'm also grateful for the opportunity to visit a rescued coyote cub at the Wildlife Discovery Center. During the summer, Mena "helped" me announce the title of this book.

My son, Keenan—I hope you recognize your qualities of leadership, wit, and inventiveness in the character of Jack.

My daughter, Mackenzie—your spunk and deep love of all God's creatures inspired Midge (and your MA studies of the suburban coyote population inspired so much of this story!).

My daughter, Megan—your resilience and your eye (both of them!) for beauty make Ruthie who she is.

My nephew-son, Patrick—your softheartedness and loyalty are embodied in Ellison.

My husband, Dan, and my immediate and extended family—you are my constant encouragers and are patient every time I begin a sentence with "How does this sound . . ." I love you!

The Moody Publishers team, editor Marianne Hering, and illustrator Aedan Peterson—so grateful to walk alongside you on the sometimes rocky, but always good, path of bringing Christ-centered books to readers.

My Super TSK Reading Team for book 2—you all deserve badges! Garrett (and his mom, Nicole), Abigail (and her dad, Ray), Maddie (and her mom, Isabel), Isaac (and his mom, Maggie); also, Josiah T., Judah and Jacob S., and Maggie and Koen.

NOTES

1. Pronounced: SOO-duh-kris TRY-ser-ee-ah-tuh.
2. Shel Silverstein, "The Edge of the World," *Where the Sidewalk Ends* (New York: HarperCollins Children's Books, 2004), 89.
3. Genesis 1.
4. "The Smells of Space: The Planets," Australian Academy of Science, February 5, 2018, https://www.science.org.au/curious/space-time/smells-space-planets.
5. This is from a study in 2007, not the 1990s when the story is set. Rehan M. Khan, Chung-Hay Luk, Adeen Flinker, Amit Aggarwal, Hadas Lapid, Rafi Haddad, and Noam Sobel, "Predicting Odor Pleasantness from Odorant Structure: Pleasantness as a Reflection of the Physical World," *Journal of Neuroscience*, September 12, 2007, https://doi.org/10.1523/JNEUROSCI.1158-07.2007.
6. Mary Bates, "Sensitive Sea Lion Whiskers Get the Job Done," *Wired*, October 1, 2014, https://www.wired.com/2014/10/sensitive-sea-lion-whiskers-get-job-done/.

7. Kate DiCamillo, *Because of Winn-Dixie*, Anniversary Edition (Somerville, MA: Candlewick Press, 2000), 57.

8. Ruthie has a condition known as *amblyopia*. When kids have this condition, one eye is weaker than the other and may turn inward.

9. Jack London, *White Fang* (New York: Scholastic, 2001), back cover copy.

10. "Repeat message," CommUSA, "Walkie Talkie '10 Codes,'" https://www.commusa.com/walkie-talkie-10-codes.

11. Jaymi Heimbuch Photography LLD, "The Urban Coyote Initiative," https://urbancoyoteinitiative.com/translating-the-song-dog-what-coyotes-are-saying-when-they-howl.

12. This is not a real book, but there are lots of good books that show you how to take care of your dog and teach it basic commands. One is *101 Dog Tricks, Kids Edition* by Kyra Sundance (Beverly, MA: Quarry Books, 2014).

13. "Light the Fire" (Bloodsmith Music, 1987). Words and music by Bill Maxwell.

14. There are different versions of this story. This one is most similar to a folktale from the Karuk people of California, First People: American Indian Legends, "How Coyote Brought Fire to the People," https://www.firstpeople.us/FP-Html-Legends/How_Coyote_Brought_Fire_To_The_People-Karok.html. A similar version, "Coyote Steals Fire for the People," retold by Alli Brydon, can be found in the book *Myths and Legends of the World*, Lonely Planet Kids (Oakland, CA: Lonely Planet Global Limited, 2019), 125–31. And another version retold by Jonathan London, called *Fire Race* (San Francisco: Chronicle Books, 1997), http://wakinguponturtleisland.blogspot.com/2010/09/coyote-steals-fire-karuk-myth.html. Here is a different

version from the Northwest Band of the Shoshone Nation: Utah State University, DigitalCommons@USU, "Coyote Steals Fire," 2005, https://digitalcommons.usu.edu/cgi/viewcontent .cgi?article=1049&context=usupress_pubs.

15. Urbanization happens when areas that are more rural, for instance, are built up into large towns or cities. Urbanization can have positive and negative effects. Study.com, "Urbanization: Lessons for Kids," https://study.com/academy/lesson/ urbanization-lesson-for-kids.html.

16. "Hine's Emerald Dragonfly," Center for Biological Diversity, https://www.biologicaldiversity.org/species/invertebrates/ Hines_emerald_dragonfly/index.html.

17. Psalm 50:10–11.

18. Jack London, *White Fang* (New York: Scholastic, 2001), 42

19. Jack London, *Call of the Wild* (New York: Scholastic, 2001), 25–26.

20. "Prowler report" and "Crime in progress," Association of Public Communications Officers, "Official Ten-Code List," last modified August 16, 2004, http://everets.org/kevin/ten-codes .php; "Trouble at this station," CommUSA, "Walkie Talkie '10 Codes,'" https://www.commusa.com/walkie-talkie-10-codes.

21. "20" stands for location. "Walkie Talkie '10 Codes,'" CommUSA, https://www.commusa.com/walkie-talkie-10-codes.

22. Cheyenne McKinley and Sarah Lower, "11 Cool Things You Never Knew about Fireflies," *Scientific American*, May 16, 2019, https://blogs.scientificamerican.com/observations/ 11-cool-things-you-never-knew-about-fireflies.

23. This isn't true, but it would be way cooler if it were. Annie Sneed, "Fact or Fiction?: People Swallow 8 Spiders a Year While They Sleep," *Scientific American*, April 15, 2014, https://

www.scientificamerican.com/article/fact-or-fiction-people-swallow-8-spiders-a-year-while-they-sleep1.

24. Gary Paulsen, *Hatchet* (New York: Simon & Schuster, 1987), 77.

25. Genesis 1:28–29, 31.

WHEN YOUR PARENTS MAKE YOUR FAMILY MOVE, IT CAN REALLY ROCK YOUR WORLD.

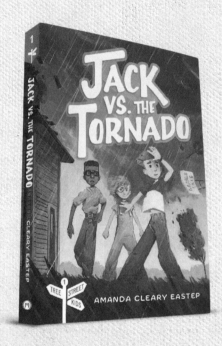

SUGAR CREEK GANG SERIES

MOODY
Publishers®

From the Word to Life®

The Sugar Creek Gang series takes you along on the faith-building adventures of some fun-loving, courageous Christian boys. These classic stories have been inspiring children to grow in their faith for over five decades. More than three million copies later, today's children can still relate to these energetic boys as they struggle to apply their Christian faith to the tumultuous adventure of life.

Also available as eBooks